LOVING LINDSEY

LOVE IN OAKTOWN BOOK 3

LARISSA GAIL

Cover Design: Wildelake Creative

Cover Image: DepositPho:os

Edited by: Anja Pfister @ HourGlassEditing

❀ Created with Vellum

OTHER BOOKS BY LARISSA GAIL

DEDICATION

In loving memory of my brother-in-law, Police Corporal John Scott Gardner, who gave his life protecting others.

CHAPTER 1

"*D*ispatch to Valley View eighty-six…"

"Dispatch to Valley View eighty-six…"

"Corporal John Miller, we thank you for your service and may you rest in peace."

Lindsey woke with a start. Holding a hand to her knotted stomach, she stared up at the streaks of morning light dancing across the ceiling. It had been months since she'd had the heart wrenching dream. The one from the awful day two years ago when she'd buried her husband, and she'd nearly broken down in front of the church full of mourners listening to dispatch give his last call at his funeral service.

But today was a new day.

The day she was going to put everything behind her.

Throwing back the white comforter she'd recently bought to replace the navy one John had picked out only a week before he'd died, the pain in her stomach eased. Lindsey stretched her arm to the side. Looking to the empty space, she smiled.

"I'm doing it, Joan. I'm getting on with my life like I promised."

Rolling over, she slid out of her lonely bed, remembering the night they'd returned from their honeymoon and John had insisted on having a conversation he deemed important. Despite her protestations, he'd broached the topic of what they should do if the unthinkable happened to either of them. As police officers both she and John understood the very real possibility either one or both of them might not come home at the end of the day. Although Lindsey hadn't wanted to talk about the subject, fearing it would put a damper on their fairytale romance, John had been adamant. And now she was glad he'd insisted. Otherwise she might still be stuck in limbo, continuing to mourn her husband like so many of her friends and family back home in Valley View, Texas.

Stretching her arms over her head, she shuffled across the carpeted floor to the window. She reached over and ran a finger along the edge of a leaf on the only surviving plant from John's memorial service resting in the center of her dresser. While she contemplated moving it to a different spot with better light in hopes of coaxing a bloom from the reluctant plant, movement in the common area of the apartments where she now lived caught her eye. She smiled as she spotted a young couple walking hand in hand down the path that wound through the tree-lined space. Watching the sweet interaction between the pair as they disappeared around the corner of one of the four buildings with units on both sides that made up the complex, John's words reverberated in her head.

"Promise me, Lindsey. Promise you'll find someone else."

"I promise, but you have to promise to do the same."

When she'd uttered those words to John she'd never in her wildest dreams thought they would come true so soon. But here she was, only four years later, facing them head on. While she still loved John with every fiber of her being, he was gone.

And it was time.

Time to forge ahead and make good on her promise. The promise to move past the devastation and get on with her life.

Later that morning, Lindsey straightened the shiny, silver badge displaying the Oaktown Police Department insignia pinned above the left pocket of her uniform shirt. Looking around the sparsely decorated, wood-paneled office she willed her wildly beating heart to slow down. She could do this.

"Anything else?"

Lindsey smiled at her new boss. "I don't think so."

"Welcome to the force, Officer Allen. Ready?"

"Thank you and yes," Lindsey replied as she got up from the plush chair in front of the glass-topped oak desk strewn with a few folders. The chief's use of her maiden name rang a bit hollow in her chest. It was necessary change, though, if she truly wanted a new start. There was always the chance someone would make the connection between her and her late husband. Her stomach twisted at the thought of anyone here looking at her with pity.

Straightening her shoulders and taking a deep breath she turned and followed her new boss out the door. Walking down the long, narrow hallway toward the training room, the rubber soles of her new work boots squeaking slightly on the polished, white linoleum, she was pleasantly surprised at the warm smiles and words of greeting from a few of her new coworkers. Smiling, and with a warm feeling bubbling up inside, she trailed behind Chief Scott as he made his way toward the front of the training room. Taking a seat in an empty spot at the end of the first row, Lindsey settled in for roll call with the Oaktown Police department.

After the chief went over the previous night's incidents, several of which involved suspected members of a gang trying to move into the area, he motioned for Lindsey. Rising, she sucked in a mouthful of air in an effort to calm the fluttering in her stomach then moved to stand next to him. Looking around, she dropped her shoulders and slowly let out her breath. Thankfully, the faces staring back at her were devoid of the pity and sadness she'd grown used to in her old department. After John had died, her former coworkers either treated her with kid gloves as if worried she might break down at any moment, while others avoided her because they were reminded of the loss of their friend and fellow officer whenever she was near. Although she'd taken back her maiden name, it wouldn't be long before her new coworkers found out she'd been married to an officer killed in the line of duty. Something she wasn't looking forward to in the least. Taking a deep breath, she smiled as Chief Scott began her introduction.

CHAPTER 2

*G*avin Thomas stared at his best friend's wife. He swallowed as Rachel's words reverberated in his head. *When was he going to get serious and settle down with someone?*

"Never, sweetheart. I'm happy with my life the way it is."

That was the easy answer. He'd always enjoyed being single and free of commitment, although lately, hooking up with a stranger hadn't held the appeal it once did. In fact, it had been three or four months since he'd been with anyone. But still, there was always a bevy of available women to warm his bed if he wanted. All he had to do was flex a muscle or flash the dimpled smile he was known for, and he'd instantly have one, if not two, beautiful women on his arm. Why would he want to tie himself down to just one? He'd seen what David had gone through with his disastrous first marriage. While his friend and coworker was in love with Rachel now, Gavin wondered how long it would last. Seemed like every time he turned around someone was splitting up with their wife or girlfriend. No, he was content with his life. He never had to worry about pleasing someone else—well, except for a few hours in bed, that is.

But he couldn't deny the twinges of longing whenever David and Rachel looked at each other. What would it feel like to have someone look at him as if he was their moon and stars?

Flinging that errant and unwelcome thought aside—hopefully far out the proverbial window in his mind—Gavin shook his head.

"Rachel, Gavin's a lady's man and nothing you say will ever change that." David chuckled as he stepped into the kitchen, giving her a kiss on the cheek. Handing over their baby daughter to Rachel, David smiled as he turned to Gavin. "Ready, Casanova?"

. . .

"Whenever you are, Captain," Gavin answered, getting up from the bench on the far side of the farm-style kitchen table. Walking around, he reached down and lightly ran a finger along the crown of Kenna's head. "See you later, princess."

When David and Rachel's baby girl gave him a toothless grin and cooed at him with her clear, bright eyes sparkling, Gavin took an awkward step back then turned and headed to the front door, trying to ignore the funny little lurch of his heart.

CHAPTER 3

"*D*ispatch to unit nineteen."

Lindsey grabbed the radio dangling from the holder on the console between herself and Officer Daniels. While she'd been on her own while on patrol back in her hometown, she was back to rookie status in Oaktown. It didn't matter how many years of experience you had when hired on at a new department, everyone started back at the beginning. Rank and tenure were earned, not handed out in the police community. Lindsey didn't mind, though. Her heart was light to be starting over where being the widow of a beloved officer wouldn't hamper her plans for advancement. She'd worked her ass off in her previous department for promotions when they came up only to be thwarted left and right by well-meaning supervisors who worried she might be too mentally fragile after what had happened to John. Tired of being passed over, and with the blessings of both her parents and former in-laws, she'd made the leap and accepted the position in Oaktown. Chief Scott had promised there would be ample opportunities to rise among the ranks as the department was currently experiencing a bevy of openings due to quite a few of the older officers reaching retirement age and a lack of new recruits. Smiling, she pressed the button on the radio.

"Unit nineteen. Go ahead dispatch."

"Unit nineteen be en route to Elm and Fourth for a ten twenty-two."

"Copy dispatch. Unit nineteen clear and en route."

Replacing the radio in its holder, Lindsey grabbed the bar above her head near the passenger door and held on as her partner for the next month or two, Sara Daniels, flipped on the lights and sirens, then made a U-turn, and headed in the opposite direction. Paying attention to the street signs and buildings they passed, trying to commit them to memory, Lindsey readied herself for her first major call as a new officer in an unfamiliar town.

As their patrol car rounded the corner of Elm Street, Lindsey took in the members of the fire department already on scene. Unbuckling her seatbelt, she exited and followed her partner to the wreckage.

She winced as the aftermath of the collision became clear. While a large, black SUV sat stalled in the middle of the intersection, a two-door, red BMW was smashed against one of the traffic lights.

Seeing no one inside the SUV, she walked toward the small group of people gathering around to watch as two firemen—one on each side of the smashed coupe—reached to open the doors to get to the injured people inside. While the driver's door opened easily and the driver was able to exit with assistance, the passenger side door resisted the rescuer's efforts.

Just as Lindsey reached the small group of observers to move them out of the way, the firefighter on the far side of the wrecked car looked up. Coming to a halt only a foot or two away from the mangled vehicle, her heart stuttered in her chest. The strong, sharp line of his jaw set off by a neatly-trimmed mustache and goatee framing a pair of full luscious lips caused a hitch in her breath. For a second or two time stood still as two stunning, brown eyes met hers across the short distance. Lindsey swallowed sharply as heat briefly flared in his gaze before the tenuous thread strung between them was broken as he looked away and called for the jaws of life.

Remembering her purpose as a first responder, Lindsey discreetly shook her head and began moving the growing crowd away from the scene before heading over to her partner. Joining Sara, she took out her notebook and pen and began questioning those who'd witnessed the accident.

As she went from person to person, gathering statements, she couldn't help but sneak more than one glance at the handsome firefighter as he worked to free the person trapped inside the car. Although he was donned head to toe in firefighter bunkers and helmet, the fact that he was in tip-top shape and probably and probably sported thick, ropy muscles underneath the heavy gear wasn't lost on Lindsey as he easily maneuvered the large rescue tool around, cutting away the metal frame of the vehicle.

A short time later, once the injured party was removed from the wreckage and Lindsey had taken the last witness statement, she looked around for the firefighter from earlier. She couldn't get his mesmerizing eyes out of her mind. Was it crazy to think she could be drawn to someone so quickly? Would John approve of her jumping in feet first? Lindsey's stomach did a funny twist, and she paused in her trek across the asphalt to the squad car. Was she just wishing too hard for someone to ease the loneliness that consumed her nights? While John had urged her to open her heart to someone else if anything happened to him, he'd also cautioned her to be sure before she jumped into a relationship.

Taking a step back toward the squad car, she shook her head. No, better to ask around about the handsome firefighter first. Plus, with her insides still feeling a little wonky perhaps she wasn't quite as ready as she thought. While her body was craving to be held by another man, she wasn't quite sure her heart was.

CHAPTER 4

"*H*ow about the student café at the high school?"

Lindsey raised an eyebrow at Sara.

"School cafeteria food? Surely there are better places to eat in Oaktown."

"Sorry, I forgot you haven't been here long. It's not the school cafeteria. The high school has a culinary arts program where students train to work in the food industry. It's really good. The instructor, Rachel Stevens, was a chef in some high-end restaurant before deciding to teach. Chief Scott likes for us to drop in once in a while to show our support and visit with the students."

Lindsey smiled at her partner. "Sure, sounds great."

While Sara radioed in to dispatch that they were taking a lunch break, Lindsey focused on the view out the windshield. She'd gotten to know her partner a little better over the three days they'd been out on patrol together. Sara, also thirty-three years old, had grown up in Oaktown and knew just about everyone, so Lindsey was hoping she could shed some light on the fireman from the other night. It wouldn't be wise to set her sights on someone who was married or had a girlfriend. Plus, Sara was divorced and recently involved in a new relationship. Although, it wasn't quite the same situation Lindsey found herself in, maybe talking to another woman would ease some of the trepidations she was facing now that following through on her promise to John was becoming a real possibility.

As Sara maneuvered the patrol car around a slow-moving van, Lindsey cleared her throat. "Can I ask you something concerning someone at the wreck the other night?"

Without taking her eyes off of the lunch hour traffic, Sara's mouth twitched. "You're going to ask me about the firefighter who helped get the passenger out of the car, aren't you?"

Lindsey's mouth dropped open. "Well, yes I was... but how'd you know?"

Sara laughed while pulling the car into the parking lot of the high school. "I saw the way you kept looking at Gavin while he worked."

As Sara parked in a spot near the front of the building, Lindsey took in a breath. So, his name is Gavin. *Well, might as well go for it,* she thought, staring straight ahead at the bricks of the school building, her heart beating wildly.

"I might have noticed him, but I need to confess something and ask your advice first. I'd like to keep this between you and me, if that's okay? Chief Scott knows, but as far as anyone else in the department, I'm not ready for them to get wind of it, yet."

Sara put the car into park and turned to Lindsey. "Sure. It's nice to have another woman on the force, and I hope we can be friends. What is it?"

"I transferred here from a small town on the other side of Dallas. My husband was John Miller. You might have heard about him. He was killed in the line of duty a couple of years ago. Anyway, we made a promise to each other that if something happened to one of us, we would move on and find someone else when the time felt right."

Lindsey closed her eyes for a second as the memory of her and John in bed the day they'd made those promises flashed in her mind. Her eyes flew back open when Sara reached over and gave her hand a squeeze.

"Yes, I remember when that happened. I'm so sorry for your loss. I'll keep it between us, but why wouldn't you want anyone to know?"

"Back in my old department everyone treated me with kid gloves. John and I graduated from the academy in Fort Worth together and were hired at the same time. We fell in love and married not too long after. John was one of those people who genuinely had

15

a good heart, and everyone loved him. When he was shot, his death shook the community. While I stayed on with the department, some of my supervisors had a hard time believing that I could handle the pressures of being promoted. I wanted to start over somewhere that I didn't have the stigma of being John's widow hanging over my head."

"That's understandable. What do you want to know?" Sara replied as she reached to quiet the radio that had started squawking.

"You're right. I did notice Gavin the other night, but I'm not sure I'm ready. I mean I thought I was, but after I got off shift and went home I couldn't get John out of my mind. I know I promised him I'd move on, and I want to…"

"But you still love him."

Lindsey nodded her head as a lone tear leaked out of one eye.

"Yes, and I always will. How am I supposed to do this?"

"Oh, honey. I wish I had a magic answer for you, but I don't. I can tell you, though, that its hard at first. When my marriage fell apart, I had no idea anything was wrong. My husband came home one day and announced he wanted a divorce. He'd been having an affair behind my back and wanted to move in with her. Needless to say, I was devasted. It took me a long time to get over him. But I did. You'll always love John, but I'm sure there's enough room in your heart to love another. You might want to consider someone besides Gavin, though."

Lindsey let out a small breath, her heart feeling a little lighter now that she'd shared her concerns with someone, only catching Sara's final words at the last second. Scrunching her brows together, she looked back to her partner.

"Why? What's wrong with him? Is he married?"

"No, he's not married, nor does he have a girlfriend, as far as I know. But Gavin's known as a player around town. He's never had a serious relationship, and at the rate he's going, he probably never will."

Lindsey's heart sank. Yeah, not exactly what she was looking for. She raised an eyebrow when Sara's lips tipped up, and she leaned across the console with a glint in her eyes.

"But, maybe that's better. Maybe you should just test the waters a little bit. See if you can handle being with someone without the pressure of wanting to get serious. But if not, I can set you up with my cousin, Rob. He's single."

Lindsey's stomach twisted. She appreciated Sara's offer to introduce her to her cousin, but there was just something about the tall, dark handsome fireman she couldn't get out of her head. She'd never been one to sleep around much, but maybe it was just what she needed. Have a little fun with Gavin before she jumped into anything serious with someone else. After all, she was new in town and no one here would care—unlike her hometown where she could barely sneeze without someone asking if she was getting sick.

Reaching over she squeezed Sara's hand. "Thanks, and maybe you're right, I'll have to think about it. Now let's go eat, and you can tell me more about Mr. Hot Fireman while I decide."

CHAPTER 5

*G*avin straightened in his chair. A smile crept over his face as the pretty police officer who'd caught his eye a few nights earlier walked through the door. He'd never seen her before that night, leading him to conclude she was new to the force. Despite the duty belt loaded down with a gun, hand-cuffs, and other gear circling her trim waist, Gavin didn't miss the way her hips swayed. Nor did the swell of her ample breasts straining underneath the bullet proof vest and dark-blue uniform shirt she wore escape his notice as she walked behind Sara Daniels on the way to a table on the other side of the crowded café.

"Earth to Gavin."

With a quick shake of his head, Gavin tore his eyes away from the heart-shaped ass of the new woman in town he had every intention of getting to know better. He turned to the guys sitting around the wooden table next to the large glass window overlooking the long hallway connecting the café to the rest of the high school. Meeting the gaze of his best friend and captain, his grin widened.

"What?"

"It never stops with you, does it?"

"Nope."

"What never stops?"

Gavin twisted around and looked for the voice coming from behind him. He smiled as David's wife, Rachel, approached the table then leaned down to give David a peck on the cheek. His heart warmed at the loving exchange between his best friend and his wife. But at the bite of jealousy that welled up inside, Gavin found his gaze once again straying to the pretty blonde with her back to him in a seat across the room. When a tinkling laugh broke through and a clear image of her greeting him with a kiss popped into his mind, Gavin shook his head and turned back to Rachel.

"Oh, I see. Want me to ask Sara to introduce you?"

Gavin playfully narrowed his eyes at Rachel. "That won't be necessary, sweetheart. I'm pretty sure I can handle it myself."

Giving his best friend's wife a wink, Gavin got up from his chair and made his way through the crowded tables. He hadn't planned to approach her while they were both on duty, but he couldn't let Rachel's comment go unchallenged. Not with the other guys as witnesses. They wouldn't give him a moments peace if he did. Reaching the table where Sara and the woman were seated, he cleared his throat surprised to find his heart beating out of his chest at the prospect of introducing himself to her.

"Oh, hey, Gavin. What's up?"

Gavin raised an eyebrow at the smirk on Sara's face informing him she understood exactly what he was up to.

"Oh, just thought I'd come over and say hi. Looks like you have a new partner," he said, walking around the corner of the table to get a better view of the beauty sitting quietly at the table.

His chest tightened and his heart skipped a beat as a pair of clear blue eyes peered up at him with curiosity. When the woman he hadn't been able to get out of his head gave him a shy smile, the noise of the crowded room faded into the background. Without hesitation, he stuck out his hand, longing to touch her smooth porcelain skin.

"Gavin Thomas."

"Hi, Lindsey Allen. Nice to meet you."

For the brief second their hands touched, a powerful surge of electricity raced up his arm and straight through his body to his dick. Tamping down the urge to sweep her up in his arms and find a private place to discover what her luscious lips tasted like, Gavin let go of her small, but surprisingly strong grip, and took a step back. Wondering at his unprecedented reaction and ignoring the slight downturn of her full lips, Gavin reminded himself he just wanted to get to know her long enough to ask her out. Hopefully he'd get a taste of what lay beneath the starched material of her uniform. He was confident once he'd had her, he'd be able to get her out of his head and move on despite the little voice in his head telling him he needed to tread carefully.

"So, how long have you been in Oaktown?" he asked, hoping to keep the conversation going long enough to figure out a way to ask for her number.

"About a week."

"How do you like Oaktown so far?"

"It's really nice. At least the little I've been able to see while moving into my apartment and starting my new job."

Gavin grinned. Unwittingly she'd just given him the perfect opening. "Would you like someone to show you around?"

"Are you offering?" she countered, grinning back up at him, causing his smile to grow even wider. Seems she was just as eager as he was to get together.

"It would be my pleasure. Are you free tomorrow?" Gavin asked, making plans in his head to take David up on his offer for a day off from is second job. He had been working from sun up to sun down the last two weeks to finish up their latest renovation on time and prove himself to the other guys on the crew.

He'd just accepted his best friend's offer to become a partner in his rapidly growing construction side-business Gavin had been helping in between his shifts at the fire department. Now that he was one of the bosses at Stevens' Construction, he could set his own schedule, so he didn't have any qualms about taking some long, overdue time off. Especially, when it came to the pretty woman smiling up at him. He would make it up to David and the crew later. A few steaks and some beer when the project was finished was a small price to pay for a little time with the gorgeous woman nodding and smiling sweetly up at him.

After exchanging phone numbers and promising to text her with a time he'd be by to pick her up the next day, Gavin didn't miss the wink Sara sent Lindsey as he turned to walk away. Ignoring the churning in his stomach at what they might be up to, he strode back across the busy café.

It didn't matter, he told himself as he returned to the table where his fellow firefighters were sitting, preparing himself for the ribbing they would undoubtedly be giving him.

CHAPTER 6

*A*fter replying to Gavin's text that he was on the way, Lindsey checked her hair one more time in the mirror. Satisfied with the soft waves she styled her long blonde hair into, she sprayed a bit of hairspray on to keep the few strands that always seemed to get in her face under control.

After swiping a hint of gloss over her lips, she smoothed down the front of her blouse. She wasn't fond of wearing button ups while off duty, but the swirling pattern of blue and green coordinated perfectly with the dark-blue fitted jeans she'd found on sale a few days prior. She hadn't been sure of what to wear, but with the weather beginning to cool down after the long, stifling Texas summer, the jeans paired with her favorite pair of ankle boots and the cotton blouse with the sleeves rolled up to her elbows seemed to be a good choice. Not too dressy and not too casual.

At a knock on her door, she wiped her sweaty palms on the hand towel hanging by the bathroom sink and took in a deep breath. Ready or not, life was about to change.

Looking through the peephole of her apartment door, Lindsey smiled at the sight of Gavin standing outside dressed in a pair of dark washed jeans and a black Henley. She let her eyes linger over the corded muscles underneath the dark skin of his forearms exposed from where he'd pushed up his sleeves. Although her hands were trembling and a lump had formed in her throat, she was determined to follow through on her plans to get on with her life. Even if nothing came of things with the handsome man on the other side of the door, she was longing to have someone hold her close once again. Like Sara said, maybe a little fling would help her ease back into dating again.

She sucked in her bottom lip. *What would John think of her choice?* Freeing her lip, Lindsey pulled back her shoulders. It didn't matter in the grand scheme of things. She deserved to be happy again. Taking a deep breath and hoping she wasn't making a mistake, she reached for the door knob.

"That was fast," Lindsey said as she swung the door open.

"I live in the building on the other side of the common area," Gavin replied. "You ready?"

"Oh, well that's convenient. I'm ready. Just let me

grab my purse and a light jacket."

Motioning for Gavin to step inside, Lindsey relaxed. Despite his reputation, the lazy smile on his face put her at ease. Sliding the strap of her cross-body purse over her shoulder and picking up her jacket, she straightened to her full height and turned back to the man she hoped would help kick-start her life on a new path.

"Ready. Where are we going to first?"

"Lunch, if that's okay. I'm starving."

Lindsey smiled as Gavin reached for the door and motioned for her to go through ahead of him.

"Sure. Sounds great."

Walking down the steps outside her apartment, Lindsey became very aware of the warm, tingling sensation shooting up and down her spine where Gavin had placed a hand on her lower back to guide her to his truck. She'd worked so hard to make it on her own the last two years that she hadn't realized how much she missed the caring touch of a man. The feel of Gavin's fingertips brushing through the fabric of her blouse and into her skin helped to loosen the tangle of knots in her stomach from worrying if she was making a mistake.

On the way to Rosalita's, the Mexican restaurant Gavin had suggested, and she'd been wanting to try, Lindsey couldn't help but laugh at the stories he told her concerning some of the goofballs he'd encountered on his shifts as a paramedic and fireman. Although sometimes a little bit macabre and more often than not sad when you stopped to think about it, joking around was one of the things that kept more than one first responder sane. Having a sense of humor about some of the stressful situations kept the tragic ones from eating away at their souls. Police, firefighters, and paramedics work hard to keep the public safe, and most people in the private sector didn't understand how they could joke about someone else's misfortune. The fact that she and Gavin had something in common to talk about eased some of the anxiety trying to creep back in when she thought about how she hoped the day might end.

After their lunch and for the rest of the afternoon, Gavin showed her around the small town. He even drove her by the gated community where Oaktown's homegrown hero, Gage Wilson and his wife, lived. Lindsey couldn't get the feeling that what they were doing was more than a hook-up and more along the lines of a first date out of her head. Sara had been adamant she not get her hopes up when it came to Gavin, and now Lindsey's thoughts were in turmoil.

She'd been prepared for a quick turn about town before trying to get her into bed, thinking it had been the reason he'd offered in the first place. But that's not what was happening at all. No, instead the handsome man with his beautiful smile, complete with an adorable dimple on one side, was pulling his jacked-up crew cab truck into a parking spot beside a tree-lined park. He was acting the exact opposite of how

Sara had described him. Making small talk and putting her at ease. Hence, Lindsey's confusion over whether this was actually a date or just a way to get into her pants. Either way, she wasn't ready for the day to end.

Lindsey jumped as the deep timbre of Gavin's voice washed over her as he put the truck into park. "How about a walk around the pond?"

"Sure. It would be nice to stretch my legs for a bit," she answered, smiling back at him as she reached for the door.

But before she could gather up her purse and jacket then turn and get out, Gavin had the door open, reaching for her hand. Placing her booted foot on the rail of the running board she placed her hand in his, marveling at how his much bigger hand swallowed hers. Lindsey stifled her gasp as large, warm fingers squeezed her own as she stepped out of the truck, sending a sharp bolt of need straight to her lady bits. When he didn't let go as he guided her to the path that ran around the edge of a sparkling pond in the center of the park, the touch of his hand in hers sent a warm buzz of pleasure through her body. Now more than ever, she hoped the day would end with her at least getting a taste of his full perfectly shaped lips, if not more. As they stepped onto the path winding around the pond, Gavin's voice broke the silence that had fallen.

"So, you mentioned you were an officer in

Valleyview, and you have family there. What prompted the move to Oaktown?"

Lindsey took a deep breath, searching for the right words. "I needed a fresh start."

"What do you mean?"

She avoided looking at Gavin in case the same pity she'd become used to was present in his gorgeous, brown eyes. "I lost my husband a couple of years ago."

She paused, glancing at Gavin. With his eyes devoid of pity and one eyebrow raised in question, she continued, "Anyway, after he died, things changed. Long story short, I'm here with my family's blessings to start over."

"I'm sorry for your loss."

Lindsey turned toward the handsome man. A feeling of relief filled her chest as his warm, comforting gaze captured hers. She sucked in a sharp breath and a tingling sensation skittered down her spine when he leaned in and said, "but I'm glad you're here now."

Her heart fluttered as he brought one hand up and tucked an errant strand of hair behind her ear. For a few seconds time stood still as they continued to look at each other. Lindsey let out a shaky breath, relieved to have the touchy subject dropped when Gavin eyes broke away and he said, "Come on. Let's keep walking."

Winding their way around to the other side of the sparkling water, Lindsey gasped as Gavin suddenly pulled her away from the path and into a copse of trees she hadn't noticed. Once inside the semi-private space, her heart gave a little flip as he backed her up against the rough bark of one of the larger trees. Her lady bits gave a shout of joy when his warm brown eyes flecked with bits of green searched hers as he angled his head and leaned in.

"Is it okay if I kiss you?" Gavin asked, running his work roughened hands up her shoulders. As his fingertips snaked into her hair, Lindsey swallowed her surprise at his question and nodded her acquiescence, her body trembling as he moved closer.

The sounds of other people walking along the path and ducks quacking as they paddled around in the water faded away when his mouth slammed onto hers. Gavin's kiss ignited a fiery response low in Lindsey's core. Unable to stop herself, she ran her hands up the hard muscles of his arms to wrap them around his neck and pull him closer.

She'd missed this. The passionate embrace of a man. Opening her mouth to the smooth, silkiness of his questing tongue, she banished all of her concerns over giving into her need and focused on the man pressing his hard, thick erect on against her stomach. Losing herself in the fiery sensations, Lindsey rubbed her throbbing core against the thigh he had pressed between her legs, desperate for release. Just as she began to tip over the edge, a loud shout from a group enjoying a round of softball in the nearby practice diamond jerked her back to reality.

Moaning at the loss of his lips and her impending orgasm, Lindsey loosened the tight grip she had on his neck as he rasped out, "Maybe we should slow down."

Putting a finger to her swollen lips, Lindsey nodded her head. *What had she been thinking?* The middle of a crowded park was no place to be intimate for the first time.

"Why don't we finish our walk around the pond?" Gavin asked, pulling his leg from between hers and stepping back.

The dimple in his cheek melted her heart a little bit more as he grinned down at her. If she wasn't careful, she was going to find herself falling for him. Probably not the best idea given his reputation around town.

"Sure," she answered, taking the hand he held out.

Stepping back onto the concrete path surrounding the pond glistening in the late evening sunlight, Lindsey cleared her throat, wanting to erase the confusion swirling around in her head. "Can I ask you a question?"

"Of course."

She swallowed hard, hoping her next words wouldn't ruin what had been building between them, but some of her previous doubts were creeping back in. A one-night stand might not be something she could live with, especially after spending the day with the handsome man beside her and getting to know him better. While her body was all for jumping into bed with Gavin to enjoy the delights of his strong, muscular body, she wasn't so sure her heart could take it. Pulling on his hand so he turned and looked down at her, she stopped walking. "What are we doing?"

"What do you mean?" he asked.

Her stomach dropped as his brows scrunched together and the corners of his mouth turned down. Lindsey took a deep breath. "I mean is this just a one-time thing or... I mean Sara told me a little about you so..."

Lindsey tried to pull her hand away as the furrow between Gain's brows deepened, and his mouth drew into a tight line. She blinked in surprise when he tightened his grip and tugged her closer. She shivered, a tingle of excitement racing down her spine when he leaned in and growled in her ear.

"Maybe you shouldn't listen to everything you hear, sweetheart." Straightening to his full height, he took her hand. "Honestly, though, I'm not sure. How about we finish our walk and then see where things go. I promise we won't do anything you don't want to."

Lindsey sighed and nodded. It wasn't the answer she wanted, but it would have to do.

CHAPTER 7

*W*ith a clang, the keys to her apartment hit the concrete landing outside her door. Lindsey closed her eyes and drew in a deep breath. As the fluttering in her stomach waned, she reminded herself this was what she wanted. She hadn't expected to be acting like a virgin about to bare herself to a man for the first time, though.

"Here, baby. I've got it."

Stepping back, she let Gavin take over getting the door unlocked. With a sweep of his hand, he motioned for her to step inside. Taking a deep breath, Lindsey crossed over the threshold. She'd had plenty of time to think as they'd walked around the pond hand in hand. While Gavin hadn't exactly answered her question, he had made it clear it was her choice if they went any further.

And it was now or never.

If she chickened out today, it would only be that much harder the next time. She'd been all in as they'd kissed in the park, but during the drive to her apartment an uncomfortable heaviness had settled in her stomach. Was she making a mistake? Was this the way to move on? Or should she wait until she found a man who would be more like John—a man confident in what he wanted and could commit to one woman?

Before she could question herself any longer, Gavin had the door shut and locked and her body pressed against one wall of her small living room. As his mouth descended on hers once again, and the heady feelings overriding everything else rose in a fiery response, she shoved aside all of her doubts. The firmness of his muscular body pressed into her own reminding her of how long she'd gone without the intimacy of being with a man.

With her pulse pounding and her body craving what Gavin was offering she moaned and leaned into his kiss. As their tongues tangled, sending sharp bolts of pleasure straight to her core, Lindsey didn't hesitate when he slid his hands down to cup her ass cheeks and lift her up. Wrapping her legs around his trim waist and her arms around his neck, she reveled in the feel of his long, thick erection as it pressed into the wet heat between her legs. When he broke the all-consuming kiss, Lindsey moaned deep in her throat at the loss of his lips.

She could only nod when he asked, "Bedroom?"

She sighed, pressing her head into the crook of his neck breathing in the soothing aroma of sandalwood mixed with the heady scent of masculinity as he carried her effortlessly down the hall.

Once he had the door open, she let go of the grip she still had around his neck and slowly slid down his tall frame, very aware of the way his cock jumped as her body rubbed against it. With a slam, Gavin kicked the door shut behind him. Lindsey closed her eyes and sighed when he wrapped his large hands around her neck, pulling her close. She sank against him as his soft, full lips pressed onto hers, and his tongue slid inside to tangle sensuously with her own.

Lost in his kiss, she moaned in disappointment when he pulled away too soon. Her heart sped up and a shiver of excitement and want raced to her core as Gavin began to unbutton her top, leaving a trail of kisses along her skin while he began to slowly undress her. As the last button was freed, she let the garment fall away to the floor, gasping loudly when Gavin pulled the lace edges of her bra down to expose her breasts, both nipples standing at attention.

A deep throaty "Yes" escaped her lips as he whispered, "So beautiful," then bent down and sucked one of the tightly puckered buds into his mouth. Lindsey's fingers fluttered over the short hair covering his head before pulling him closer, pushing her chest toward him as he released the thoroughly ravished tip and moved to the other. She threw her head back, reveling in the scorching heat building in her lower body as he continued to suck and nip both of her nipples in turn. After what seemed like an eternity, Gavin pulled away, placing a quick kiss on each rosy-red tip. Smiling Lindsey looked down into his handsome face. Her clit throbbed with need and her heart swelled at the hungry look in his dark, hooded eyes.

Swallowing in anticipation of what she would find, Lindsey reached out and slowly released the buttons on the front of Gavin's shirt. Once the last button popped open, she ran her hands up the muscular tautness of his chest, her fingers tingling in the fine dusting of black hair spread across the broad expanse. Breaking eye contact, she leaned forward to lay soft kisses along his skin until she reached one of his dark, tight nipples. Embolden by the hoarse sound escaping his throat, she circled the tight buc with her tongue. As he dug his fingers deeper into her hair, she trailed her lips to the other side. After giving that nipple a quick nip and suck, she pulled away and looked up. The heat and longing she could see in his eyes sent her heart soaring. It had been so long since she'd had a man look at her as if he wanted to devour her that all her earlier hesitation fled her mind. She wanted him. The heat and desire coursing through her body far surpassing anything or anyone before.

Grinning, she dropped down to her knees on the carpeted floor, wanting to get a taste of the long, thick length poking at her through his jeans.

"You don't have to," Gavin said, catching hold of her chin to tip her head up as she reached for his belt.

"Please, I want to," she pleaded, looking up at him imploringly.

With a chuckle, he let go of her chin and helped her with the silver contraption and buttons on his jeans. "Wouldn't want to deny you anything, sweetheart."

Wetness pooled between her legs as Gavin hooked his thumbs in the waist of his jeans and the snug boxers underneath then slid them over his hips. As his heavy, thick cock sprung free from its confines, her pussy clenched and her mouth watered in anticipation.

Reaching out, she touched the precum oozing from the bulbous head. She smiled at the low groan Gavin let out as she licked the salty wetness from her fingertip. Grasping the base of his hard length, Lindsey slid her lips over and down the velvety softness of his shaft. She opened her mouth wide and pushed forward. Swallowing against her gag reflex as his cock hit the back of her throat, she slowly began sucking and licking up and down the hard length. She loved the way Gavin reached down and placed one hand on the back of her head, urging her to keep up the rhythm she set, her pussy clenching in anticipation with every stroke of her tongue. Just as Gavin's cock pulsed and began to swell, he pushed her head away. Letting go, she looked up and smiled at the deep husky tone of his voice when he said, "Even though that feels incredible, I'd rather come inside you."

As he toed off his black vans and then stepped out of his jeans and boxers, another shiver of need and want race down Lindsey's spine straight to her clit. She squealed in surprise when he picked her up and tossed her onto the bed before quickly divesting her of the skinny jeans and her lacy thong underwear.

Her heartbeat ramped up at the growl in Gavin's throat, and she raised herself up on her elbows as he crawled between her legs, pushing her thighs apart to spread her wide.

She watched as a grin spread over Gavin's face when his fingers slid through her wetness and parted her folds. Throwing her head back, she moaned loud and long as the first swipe of his tongue met with her clenching center, nearly sending her over the precipice. When his tongue slowly circled her clit, her hips began to undulate of their own accord driving her mad with desire.

Lifting her head, she rasped out in a voice she barely recognized, "Please."

With a chuckle, Gavin met her gaze then reached out with his tongue to flick back and forth across, the tip of her pulsing nub. With a hissed, "Yes," she collapsed back against the cool cotton of the bedding, letting the waves of her first orgasm in a long time—from something other than her own hands—wash over her. When the blinding lights behind her eyelids began to fade and the sound of a condom wrapper being opened broke through the leftover haze of her pleasure,

Lindsey smiled and opened her eyes. The heated passion in Gavin's eyes as he rolled the latex down his hard length was enough to send another bolt of desire to her core.

Not wanting to wait a moment longer, Lindsey reached out and wrapped her hand around his warm, hard length. Her clit pulsed with the need to have him pushing inside to fill her long-neglected center.

"A little eager, are we?" he rasped, causing a blush to creep up her neck.

She released his thickness and moaned as he dipped his head and took one of her aching nipples in his mouth. At the pull of his mouth on the sensitive bud, she wrapped her arms around his shoulders and pulled him in closer. Digging her nails into the smooth, silky skin of his back she urged him on in a silent plea. To her relief, Gavin let go of the aching peak and reached down to position his cock against her dripping folds.

"Ready, baby?"

With a quick nod, she wrapped her legs around his middle and moaned as he slowly pushed inside. The feel of his cock as it spread her wider than she'd ever been before was indescribable. When he planted himself as deeply as he could, the walls of her pussy clenched and she gasped. As he pulled back and then slid back in, Lindsey pressed her heels into his back and rocked her hips, matching his rhythm. Almost instantly, she became lost in the undulating waves of pleasure coursing through her body while her core tightened around him and bright lights exploded behind her eyes. She didn't know if it was simply because it had been so long or if it was something more. But she knew once wasn't going to be nearly enough with the beautiful man smiling down at her, the dimple in his cheek spurring on the last pulses as his magnificent cock moved languidly inside her.

CHAPTER 8

*G*avin scowled down at the plywood panel he'd just cut into the wrong length. What the hell was wrong with him? He'd never been this conflicted after sleeping with a woman before. Maybe it was the fact he'd done something he rarely ever did— stayed the night. Although he'd made a quick exit that morning with no promises of anything more, he couldn't get his mind off the beautiful blonde and her hot, sweet pussy.

They'd made love several times. *Whoa, there. Made love?* When had he ever considered it making love? She was messing with his head. While he sometimes found himself envying his best friend and the life he had with Rachel, Gavin wasn't sure he was ready to settle down like David had. He loved women—all types—although lately, for some unknown reason, he found himself turning down the ones who approached. The very ones he would have happily jumped in bed with for a few hours of fun a few months ago.

But something about Lindsey was different.

And what did it mean that she was the first in several months to get his dick working again? Why was she so different? Was she someone he could... His thoughts trailed off as footsteps crunched on the gravel walkway behind him.

"Long night?"

Gavin turned to his best friend as he came up beside the table saw where he'd been staring off into space in the early morning light.

"Yeah, didn't get back to my apartment until this morning."

"So, I take it things went well with your date?"

"Wasn't a date. I was just showing her around town," Gavin growled, tossing the useless piece of lumber to the side, bemoaning the fact he'd simply planned on taking Lindsey for a spin around town before seducing her only to find himself not wanting the day to end. Picking up another piece of plywood, he laid it on the flat surface of the saw, scowling at his best friend as David's shoulders shook with mirth.

"Better be careful or you might find yourself falling for this one."

Gavin scowled at the crinkle around David's eyes and the grin on his face. "Just trying to be nice."

"Whatever you say, man. I'm just calling it like I see it."

Gavin pushed the large panel of plywood up to the sharp blade, making sure to line up to the correct marks this time. Reaching down, he flipped the switch on and proceeded to cut the wood, drowning out David's loud guffaws of laughter as he walked off.

After turning off the saw and hefting the correctly cut piece of wood onto his shoulder, Gavin headed back into the gutted house, contemplating staying away from the blonde and her seemingly magic pussy that had him thinking about things he'd never wanted before. Maybe a night out at the Buckin' Bull to hook up with one of the willing pieces of ass he could always find there now that he was back in action would do the trick. Anything to get the image of Lindsey and her sweet pussy out of his head.

CHAPTER 9

*L*indsey shook her head as Sara pulled their patrol car to a stop at a red light. "What?"

"I asked how your, dare I say, date with Gavin went?"

Lindsey stared at her partner. Had it been a date? She was so confused. She understood from what Sara had told her that Gavin didn't date, preferring to hook up with any of the variety of willing woman he had at his disposal. But it sure had seemed like a date. Sara had said he might ask a girl out but with the clear understanding it wouldn't go any further than a night or two.

And the sex? Out of this world. She wasn't going to give her heart away that easily, though. Not with a man who was known to be a player. No, better to forget about him and move on to someone else. Besides, she wasn't in a hurry. She was going to heed John's words and take her time to make sure before she jumped into another relationship. Even if the sex with Gavin had been unbelievable, and she was already yearning for a connection with him. No, she'd be better off with someone more like John. Someone not afraid of commitment.

"It was okay," Lindsey answered with a blush creeping up her neck.

"Okay?" Sara raised her eyebrow and bounced in her seat. "Oh, my goodness. You slept with him. Now you've got my attention. Was he any good?"

"Well, pretty good," Lindsey answered, slumping down in her seat.

"Just pretty good? From what I've heard Gavin is a stud between the sheets," Sara remarked as she looked over and winked at Lindsey. "Is he as big as they say?

The tinge of pink climb higher. Ducking her head, she looked down to her hands as she fiddled with the buckle of her duty belt. She wasn't one to talk about her sex life, but Sara seemed to be open-minded. Maybe if she could talk about it she'd be able to figure out what to do concerning the conflicted emotions she was having about Gavin.

"Bigger than I've ever had. Of course, that's not saying much, since besides John I've only been with a couple of other guys."

Smiling, Lindsey looked down at the juncture of her thighs remembering the delicious feel of Gavin's huge cock sliding in and out between them bringing her to orgasm over and over. Blushing she glanced over to find Sara looking back at he with an enormous grin on her face.

"That good, huh?"

"Yeah. He made me come so many times it's a wonder I can even walk today." Lindsey bit her lip at the wide-eyed look Sara was giving her. "Too much information?"

"No, not at all," Sara answered, moving her eyes back on the road as the traffic light turned green. "I'm just surprised he stayed the night. Usually, once or twice and it's over with him. At least that's what I've been told."

"Oh."

Lindsey didn't know what to think, her confusion increasing. Sara's reaction confirmed the feeling she'd had all along that he had acted differently with her. Could she dare hope he might want something more or would she end up hurt? On the other hand, maybe she should explore some other options before she got her hopes up about someone who was known for not committing.

Staring at her laptop screen later that evening as she lay in bed, Lindsey took a deep breath and hit enter. With the wonky shifts she'd been working at the police department the last few days, and the lack of eligible men in Oaktown, she'd decided to try her hand at online dating. Along with offering up a blind date with her cousin, which Lindsey was considering, Sara had also recommended the dating site she'd met her current boyfriend on as an option. Now all Lindsey had to do was wait. Maybe a nice man interested in pursuing a relationship would respond. While she liked Gavin, the fact that he'd slept around with so many other women didn't sit well with her. Not that she needed to worry about it since he hadn't attempted to contact her after he'd shown her around town and then screwed her brains out. What Sara had warned her about him was turning out to be true, and she was better off without him.

Ding!

Well, that was fast, she thought as the picture of a good-looking man in a navy polo popped up on her screen. Reading through the man's message and profile, Lindsey smiled and began typing out a response. Maybe it wasn't going to be as hard as she'd thought it would be to find someone with the same interests and goals.

CHAPTER 10

Gavin looked across the dance floor as he twirled the bottle of Shiner between his fingers. He'd come to the Buckin' Bull to enjoy a few beers with David and Gage, both of whom had already left to go home to their wives. In the past, he would have already set his sights on the first pretty girl to look his way, but a certain blue-eyed beauty kept invading his thoughts.

With a sigh, he set the nearly empty bottle of beer on the high-top table and stood up with the intent of leaving and going back to his apartment—alone. However, a glimpse of a familiar blonde coming through the door of the popular bar stopped him in his tracks. Taking his seat once again, he raised a finger at one of the waitresses motioning for her to bring him another beer. Relaxing against the wooden back of his stool, he watched as Lindsey made her way through the crowd to the bar that took up most of one wall of the rough-timbered building.

After a few days of mulling things over, he still hadn't decided how to proceed. He'd wanted to ask her out again to see if the attraction between them was as strong the second time around, but between working late hours on the renovation site and taking an overtime shift at the fire station time had gotten away from him. His dick swelled against the zipper of his jeans at the thought of holding her close and burying himself in her luscious body once again.

His calm demeanor soon shifted, though, when a moron dressed in a pair of khaki pants, light-blue polo shirt, and a pair of gray vans—totally out of place in the western atmosphere of the bar—placed a hand on her shoulder. An angry tick set up in his jaw as he watched Lindsey flash a brilliant smile and turn around to grab the asshole's hand and drag him along behind her. With an unfamiliar wave of jealousy along with a dull thud in his chest, Gavin plastered a smile he didn't quite feel on his face and crooked a finger at the pretty, dark-haired girl in a pair of tight-fitting jeans and crop top who'd been giving him googley eyes since he'd sat down to come over. If Lindsey wanted to play that game he could, too. Never mind that she was perfectly in her rights to go out with someone else.

Forcing his eyes away from Lindsey and the asshole she was with, Gavin patted the bar stool at his side. As his new conquest plopped herself up on the seat beside him, he resisted the urge to stomp over and slam his fist into the face of the other man touching the smooth, silky skin of Lindsey's hand. While he watched from the corner of his eye as she and her date made their way through the crowd, he sternly told himself Lindsey had just saved them both from a world of hurt. It never would have worked out. She was too good for him—a man with a reputation he'd probably never live down.

Turning his back so that the visage of wavy blonde hair and stunning blue eyes moved out of sight, he leaned over and smiled at the pretty brunette.

"Hey, baby. What's your name?"

"Stephanie."

Gavin blew out a breath, not quite sure why the brunette's perkiness felt more like an irritation than a turn on. Usually the energetic response of a girl clearly itching to hop into bed would have his dick standing at attention. The more enthusiastic the better. But for some inexplicable reason his cock deflated behind his zipper. *Maybe a turn around the dance floor would get things moving along,* he thought as he held out his hand.

"How about a dance?"

"Sure."

He inwardly winced at her giggled reply but sucked it up and led Stephanie onto the scuffed dance floor just as a two-step song started. He let out a sigh of relief when Lindsey and her date began to make their way to a table in the far back corner opposite the stage where the local country band was playing. *Out of sight, out of mind.*

He hoped.

A bit later, after a few more spins around the dance floor, he still wasn't feeling it any more than he had been when he'd called Stephanie over. In fact, the touch of her fingers trailing up and down his shoulders as they'd slow danced had his balls shriveled up to nothing.

Needing to piss like a son-of-a-bitch, he guided the flushed brunette back to the high-top table. After making sure she had a glass of water to cool her down after whirling her around the dance floor more times than he should have trying to get a response out of his wayward dick, he hightailed it to the men's room down the back hallway.

As he relieved himself, Gavin tried to think of a way to ditch Stephanie. He couldn't believe he was going to give up the easy pussy so freely offered, but he found he couldn't stomach the thought of taking her to bed.

Zipping up his pants, he headed out the door. Being careful to stay out of sight of the brunette still sitting on top of the bar stool across the room where he'd left her, Gavin quickly settled his tab and made his way through the heavy, rough-hewn oak door to the parking lot. Once Stephanie realized he wasn't coming back, he was confident she'd find someone else to hook up with while he did something that would have been unusual in the past—go home alone.

Walking across the parking lot, listening to the crunch of gravel underneath his boots, his ears perked up as the sound of a struggle broke through his thoughts of *what the hell was the matter with him.*

When a loud slap rent through the air and a man's voice shouted, "You, bitch!" Gavin found himself running toward a long line of trucks and cars parked along the back edge of the lot. As he raced around a mid-sized SUV, his heart took a tumble at the sight of Lindsey, blood dripping from one side of her face, leaning forward against the side of the vehicle. Reaching out he grabbed her elbow and turned her around.

"What happened? Are you okay?" he asked, reluctantly drawing his hand away from her silky skin, telling himself the cut on her temple wasn't as bad as it looked. Head wounds tended to bleed worse than others.

"Yeah. I'm fine. The bastard thought he could get away with feeling me up right here in the parking lot," she answered as she brushed off the bits of gravel stuck to her form-fitting jeans highlighting the fullness of her ass, ignoring the blood running down the side of her face.

Cracking his knuckles and flexing his biceps, Gavin contemplated going after the sorry asshole he could see holding his junk and hobbling over to a flashy sports car. The urge to pound the guy's sorry ass into the ground coursed through his body. With a low growl in his throat, Gavin clenched his fists and turned back to Lindsey.

"Are you going to press charges? Assholes like that need to know they can't go around groping women without their consent."

Lindsey took a deep breath while a flush of pink crept up her neck in the soft glow of the street light overhead. Gavin tensed knowing he wasn't going to like her answer.

"No, but I warned him I'd be keeping an eye on him, and if he did it to another woman, I'd let the chief know what happened."

At another low growl emanating from Gavin's chest at her reply, Lindsey reached out and put her hand on his arm. "Hey. Calm down, big fellow. I can take care of myself. I got him pretty good in the nuts."

Gavin scraped a hand over the coarse hair on his chin, his ire softening a bit from Lindsey's words and the soft touch of her hand on his arm. She was a police officer and was no doubt trained in the art of self-defense and probably embarrassed she'd let the asshole get his hands on her. He couldn't help but worry, though, that she was injured more than she was letting on when she brought the fingers of her hand up to the cut on her temple and winced.

"Here. Let me take a look."

CHAPTER 11

D *arn it!*

The last thing Lindsey needed was to end the horrible night with Gavin. He obviously didn't want a relationship—not after she'd seen him with the cute, brown-haired girl inside the bar. The way they'd had their hands all over each other while they twirled around to song after song had assured her the two would end up in bed together before the night was through. Best to get rid of him and then go home to soak in a warm bubble bath to try and forget about her disastrous evening and the pounding in her head.

"That's all right. I'll be fine."

"I'm sure you will be, but it will make me feel better if you let me check. Even though I drive the fire engine, I'm still a certified paramedic," Gavin said, one side of his full lips tipping up. He took a step closer—that darn dimple in his cheek doing funny things to her insides.

Lindsey took a deep breath, willing her racing heart to stop fluttering so wildly beneath her ribs. It wouldn't do to let him know how he affected her when he was so close, the warmth of his muscular body causing a skittering cascade of desire to sweep over her.

"Okay, but what about the girl that you were dancing with? Won't she be wondering where you are?"

"I'm sure she'll latch onto someone else when she realizes I'm not coming back. Besides, I'm not going anywhere until I know that moron is gone," he said, nodding toward the sound of tires squealing on the asphalt.

Lindsey's breath hitched as Gavin took her chin in one hand then raked back her hair with the other. When he leaned in closer to inspect the cut on her head her knees almost gave out. The minty freshness of his breath mixed with the faint smell of beer washed over her skin. Slowly, the pounding in her head began to decrease. She shivered, remembering his powerful embrace from only a short week ago.

"The bleeding is slowing down, but that cut looks pretty nasty. What did he hit you with anyway?"

Lindsey looked up, trying to focus on Gavin's warm gaze. Her vision was a little blurry from the altercation she'd had with her date. Although it hadn't been a solid blow, she'd managed to knee him in the balls after he'd hit her across the temple in response to her slap when he'd tried to pin her against her car and grope her breasts. Luckily, he'd only grazed her head.

"He was wearing a college ring. It must have caught my skin when he backhanded me."

"That bastard. Why some men don't believe *no* means *no* I'll never understand. You sure you're okay, baby? Your eyes look a little fuzzy."

A shiver of warmth ran up Lindsey's spine at his endearment. Why did he have to call her baby? It made her want to curl up in his arms and let him take care of her. But she couldn't allow it. Jerking her chin out of his grasp, she stepped back only to stumble as her boot hit a patch of loose gravel. She tipped sideways and the pain in her head roared back to life. Two strong arms reach out to break her fall. Before she could react, Gavin had her cradle up against his chest, taking long strides across the parking lot.

"Put me down," she cried, struggling to get out of his grip.

"No. You're in no condition to drive. I should take you to the hospital, but—"

Lindsey didn't let him finish. "No," she admonished. "I'm feeling better. You can put me down." The last thing she needed was for the other officers at the department to know she'd almost been taken advantage of. She didn't want them to think she wasn't capable of taking care of herself in volatile situations. Perhaps if she'd stalked the guy's social media a little closer, or asked around about him, she would have discovered something in his past that would have made her hesitate to accept a date with him. As it was, she could kick herself for letting him get the better of her and just wanted to go home and lick her wounds. But if she caught wind of him doing it to someone else, she'd put that embarrassment aside and march right into the chief's office and let him know what had happened.

"Not a chance, sweetheart."

"Fine," Lindsey huffed as Gavin came to a stop next to his truck.

She held onto his neck while he reached into his pocket to grab his keys. After hitting the unlock button and grabbing the door handle to open the passenger side door, he gently sat her down in the seat.

"What are you doing?" she asked as he reached for the seatbelt, his muscled arm brushing across her breasts to send a sharp spike of need straight to her center.

"Taking you home. No way am I letting you drive."

"What about my car?"

"You can take care of it tomorrow. Now quit asking questions so I can get you back to your apartment, take care of that cut, and make sure you're going to be all right."

Lindsey sighed, not completely sure what Gavin was up to. She was too tired to argue, though. She'd let him get her home, check her out, then make sure he left. No hanky-panky this time. Letting herself fall for the gorgeous fireman would only lead to heartbreak.

"Ouch."

"Sorry, but I need to make sure this doesn't get infected," Gavin said, swiping the cut on the side of Lindsey's head with a cotton ball and some peroxide. "Almost done."

Lindsey held in a sigh as Gavin's deep soothing voice slid over her. The pain in her head was decreasing by the minute, but to her consternation a deep throbbing coil of need was beginning to build in her core. Seems getting a small taste of the man standing between her legs while she sat on the bathroom counter letting him take care of her hadn't been enough. Biting her lip, she kept her eyes to the floor while he placed a couple of butterfly strips on her injury.

"There. All done."

Keeping her eyes averted, knowing she'd give into the temptation to kiss him if she looked at him, she held her breath, waiting for him to step back. Her breath hitched and a flood of warmth filled her chest when instead he reached out with one hand to grasp her chin and tilt her head up. His warm, tender gaze sent her heart skittering. When he leaned in and swept his lips across hers, she let the trepidations of how she would feel when he went on to his next conquest go. Wrapping her arms around his neck and her legs around his waist, she allowed him to lift her up and carry her to the bedroom. Seems she couldn't resist the explosive way her body responded whenever they touched.

One more time won't hurt, she reasoned.

Without preamble they both began to tear frantically at their clothing, what happened earlier forgotten. Once they were both naked and a condom had been retrieved from Gavin's pants pocket, he had her pressed into the mattress with his magnificent cock spreading her wide. Her walls pulsed in pleasure around the hard thickness slowly pressing inside. Moaning, she pulled his head down to one breast. As he sucked and nipped at the sensitive tip, Lindsey met the pounding thrusts of his rhythm.

Once the racking waves of an orgasm began to rock through her core, she opened her eyes. Her heart fluttered at the sight of the magnificent man above her throwing his head back to roar out his release.

Collapsing down on one elbow, Gavin pulled her close and rolled to the side. Tucking her head into the crook of his neck and breathing in the sandalwood and sweaty musky scent that belonged uniquely to the man she was wrapped up in, Lindsey let out a long slow breath. The feel of his arms wrapped around and holding her close helped to ease the heartbreak she'd been carrying for the last two years.

John had been right. She couldn't live without someone to hold her tight. Although she could be tough when necessary, especially in her role as a police officer, she'd also grown up in a loving family and needed that connection. While her parents and brother would be there if she needed them, it wasn't the same as being close to someone who held your soul in their hands. John had been that for her, but he was gone.

Although the fiery need coursing between them wouldn't last, it felt like heaven to be held close by Gavin. With a sigh, she let go of the deep-seated tension she'd held onto for far too long and snuggled closer.

CHAPTER 12

*G*avin woke with a start. The strange feeling of a pair of soft hands stroking up and down his straining cock almost had him shooting out of bed. But when he looked down to see Lindsey peering up at him with a lazy grin on her face, he relaxed. He'd never felt this way before. Rather than itching to leave, he wanted nothing more than to spend more time with her. With that new and unfamiliar thought swirling in his mind, his chest filled with warmth while taking in the beautiful woman now wrapping her luscious lips around his cock.

Closing his eyes, Gavin laid back and let her tongue work its magic. When his balls drew tight and his cock began to swell, he reached down and grabbed a handful of blonde hair and pushed Lindsey's warm, wet mouth all the way down on his throbbing shaft. Thrusting once, then twice, he threw his head back and grunted, spewing his release into her mouth. Jackknifing up after she licked the last drops from his dick, he smiled and flipped her over onto her back pressing himself against the junction of her thighs, his dick nowhere near satisfied.

Scooting down the bed, Gavin pushed Lindsey's legs apart, exposing the bright, pink petals of her sex glistening with arousal. Dipping his head, he let the sweet taste of her honeyed juices flow over his tongue. As she moaned and let her head roll back onto the jumble of pillows, Gavin began to tease at her clit. Once her hips began to rock against his face, he slipped two fingers into her heat. With renewed fervor, he flicked the tip of his tongue around and over her throbbing nub. His name passing through her lips in a low wail at the height of her orgasm caused a hitch in his breath and an odd tightness in his chest.

"Wow. I could get used to waking up like this."

"You like that, baby?" Gavin answered, ignoring the battling voices in his head. One telling him he was making a mistake and the other urging him on. The desire to hold the beautiful blonde looking at him with hunger in her clear blue eyes won out. Kissing a path up her heated body, Gavin positioned himself at her entrance. "Want more?"

At the slight nod of her head, he reached over to grab a condom from the nightstand. After sheathing himself, he slid his throbbing cock deep inside her clenching walls. The feel of her smoothness as she clenched around him almost sent him slipping over the edge too soon. Wanting to take it slow and savor the woman wrapped around him, Gavin dipped his head and took her mouth. With long deliberate strokes, Gavin pounded into her until she began to pulse around him.

Later that morning, Gavin watched as Lindsey pulled out of the bar's parking lot. The fact that he hadn't let her know what he was feeling settled like a lump of coal in his gut. She was probably wondering what was going on, but something made him hold back. He didn't like the wayward thoughts his mind had turned to—stupid things like marriage and a house full of babies that he'd never had desired before. She'd been through a devastating loss and the last thing he wanted to do was hurt her.

What if things didn't work out?
What if she wasn't feeling the same?

CHAPTER 13

*L*indsey tucked the bottom of her navy-blue uniform shirt into her pants then fastened the buckle on her duty belt. Double checking that her service revolver was securely seated in its holster, she grabbed her keys and headed out the door.

It was going to be a long night on patrol trying to avoid Sara's questions about her date. She didn't have a problem letting her know about the handsy bastard she'd kicked in the nuts. It was what had happened *after* she wasn't quite sure how to explain. Sara had tried to warn her about Gavin, but one look in his brown eyes and the touch of his hands had sent all her reasons for not falling prey to his wiles once again out the door.

· · ·

She'd promised herself after the first time she wouldn't let herself get caught up in hoping for more from him when he was only after a good time. In her defense, though, the previous night was all on him. He could have simply seen her home, made sure she was okay, and then left. But no...Mr. I-Have-a-Cock-You-Can't-Resist couldn't let things be. One swipe of his glorious lips against hers, and she was a goner.

Although John would probably be proud of her for going after something she wanted, he darn sure wouldn't approve of Gavin. With his reputation preceding him, Gavin more than likely wouldn't stick around no matter how much she was beginning to wish he would.

Maybe she should accept Sara's offer to set her up with her cousin. He couldn't be any worse than the guy she'd so unwisely picked from the online dating site. Anything to get her mind off the tall, handsome firefighter and his magic cock.

"Well?"

· · ·

Lindsey bit the inside of her lip. She ran her hands over the scratchy fabric of her pants, trying to think of something to change the subject. Coming up empty-handed, she sighed then shrugged her shoulders.

"That bad, huh?"

"It wasn't great," Lindsey conceded.

"Oh, honey. I'm sorry. Want to talk about it?"

Lindsey gritted her teeth and looked over at her partner as Sara eased the patrol car into the heavy traffic. She didn't have anyone else to confide in, so why the hell not?

"My date turned out to be an asshole."

"What do you mean? I thought you were going to check out his social media."

. . .

"No, I decided not to and that was my first mistake. He was all right to begin with. Actually, pretty funny and easy to talk to. That is until the night wore on and he'd downed a couple of beers."

"Oh no. What happened?" Sara cried as she pulled the patrol car into the parking lot of the shopping center to circle around and look for any suspicious behavior.

"After dinner, we went to the Buckin' Bull. We had a couple of drinks and danced a bit. When I said I was tired and ready to go, he seemed amicable enough until we hit the parking lot. Before I knew it, he had me backed up against my car with his hand up my shirt."

Sara's mouth dropped open. Shaking her head, she slowly began to drive around to the back of the strip of buildings housing a donut shop, a hair salon, and pack and ship store. "Surely you put him in his place."

"Of course," Lindsey replied taking in the outrage evident on her partner's face. She pressed her lips together and pulled her hair back on one side to expose the bandages Gavin had placed on her cut. "But not before he backhanded me and snagged my temple with his ring."

"Did you file charges? I didn't see any at the station."

"No. But rest assured, I'll be reporting him to the dating sites I find his profile on."

Lindsey turned to the window to scan for anyone seemingly out of place while Sara drove slowly through the darkened alley behind the pack and ship store that had been broken into a few nights before.

"There's more to this story, isn't there?" Sara asked, turning the wheel to maneuver out of the alley and back onto the street.

Once again, Lindsey bit into her lip. It was amazing how quickly she and Sara had become in tune with each other. She'd noticed when Sara had been off a few days ago after having an argument with her boyfriend. In return, Sara could tell something was bothering her. Riding around together in such a tiny space with nothing else to do but talk had them both aware when something was upsetting the other. Better to tell her now instead of having to endure repeated questions the rest of their shift.

"I might have done something I shouldn't have."

"Go on."

"Well, when Jeremy hit me he nearly knocked me out, but I managed to knee him in the balls. Another reason I didn't chase after him and arrest him. Luckily, Gavin happened to be there and came over to help."

"Oh, tell me more," Sara crooned, her eyes crinkling in amusement.

Wringing her hands, Lindsey looked down to her lap and took a deep breath. "I might have had sex with Gavin again."

"Oh, don't give me that. You either did or you didn't."

· · ·

"Okay, we did," Lindsey confessed, feeling the blush on her neck creeping up to her cheeks.

"Good for you. You're a single woman. There's no shame in having a little fun," Sara said.

Lindsey looked to her partner. "It's not that. I'm confused to say the least. He stayed the night then took me for breakfast before taking me to get my car."

"He did what?"

"You heard me. After I got over my unease of having a one-night stand, here he is acting all concerned and shit. I think I'm starting to have feelings for him and—"

"Oh, honey. I'm not sure that's wise," Sara interrupted. "As I said before, he's not the settling down type. Although it is curious why he's coming back for more."

"Exactly my point. Before Jeremy and I left the bar, he was dancing with a girl. The way they were hanging on to each other I assumed he would be hooking up with her. But when he helped me she was nowhere to be seen."

"Hum. Maybe 'Mr. I Don't Want a Relationship' is changing his ways. Did he say anything about seeing you again?" Sara asked.

"No."

"Well, I wouldn't read much into it then. Maybe he just wanted to get you in bed again. A girl can't turn a handsome man like that down, can she?" Sara teased before she pulled into the Whataburger drive-thru.

"No, you're right. He's irresistible," Lindsey answered, more confused than ever.

If all he wanted was another romp in the sack then why did he stay in her bed holding her close? He could have easily left after they'd done the deed and gone his merry way. And why did he insist on taking her for breakfast and carrying on a conversation, asking her all kinds of things like he wanted to get to know her? She was going to have to be very careful the next time she ran into him. If she wasn't, she was going to fall for the handsome man and that would never do.

Not when she wanted a stable relationship with a man who *would* stick around.

CHAPTER 14

avin watched his best friend lift his son, Kyle, into the driver's seat of the fire engine. His heart gave a little twist at the sight of the little boy's face lighting up in a huge grin when he honked the horn. Then, when Kimmie, Kyle's twin, tugged on the back of David's uniform and giggled "Me next, Daddy" an unfamiliar tightness set up in his chest. He'd thought about what he was missing out on not settling down with a woman and starting a family once or twice but had always quickly dismissed the idea. He'd kept reminding himself he was content with his life, not having to worry about keeping up with a house and all that entailed and trying to keep a woman and kids happy. But was he?

"Uncle Gavin. Uncle Gavin. Watch this."

Gavin shook his head and turned to watch Kimmie honk the horn then twist the steering wheel of the huge truck, pretending to drive. The sound of her giggles and the sight of her sweet cherubic face had Gavin wondering what his kids would have looked like if he'd chosen to go down that path. He shook his head to clear the image of a little girl with dark curls forming in his brain. *Don't go there*, he admonished himself then took a couple of steps over to lift Kimmie from the seat of the truck where she continued to press on the button of the loud blaring horn.

"That's enough, sweetheart. Don't want the neighbors to turn us in for disturbing the peace."

The second the words were out of his mouth, he smiled at the picture in his head of Officer Allen pulling up to investigate the complaint. Unlike so many of the other women he'd enjoyed, he couldn't get her out of his mind. Usually, once he'd fucked someone, he could go about his business and not give them a second thought. But not, it seemed, with the gorgeous blonde officer and the instant connection he'd felt with her. They had a lot in common, both being first responders with an innate desire to help others. It was a refreshing change from the women who threw themselves at him solely based on his looks.

"Earth to Gavin."

David's booming laughter jolted Gavin out of his thoughts. Placing Kimmie on his hip, he turned around.

"What?" he snapped, perturbed he'd been caught daydreaming about Lindsey once again.

"I asked if you were ready to take this inside. The guys probably have everything set up by now."

"Sure," Gavin answered, following David through the door leading from the large garage into the living area of the station. He watched his best friend carry Kyle in one arm while wrapping another arm around his wife as she carried their baby daughter, Kenna. While he walked behind the loving couple to the small celebration set up for the twins since David had to be on duty at the fire station on their birthday, Gavin couldn't help but be reminded of all he was missing out on.

"You seem awfully quiet today," Rachel remarked as she sat down next to him at the long wooden table in the firehouse kitchen.

"Just have a lot on my mind." Gavin shrugged while he handed a plate with a slice of cheese pizza on it to Kimmie who'd insisted on sitting next to her 'Uncle Gavin'.

With the guys talking in the background and Kimmie and Kyle opening up a few presents, Gavin's mind wandered back to Lindsey. Did the fact that he couldn't seem to get her off his mind mean something? A streak of longing flashed through his chest at the loving way David stroked Rachel's arm while everyone watched the twins rip the paper off yet another gift. Was he truly happy? Standing by his best friend's side as he went through hell with his witch of an ex-wife, Gavin had been reassured staying single was the way to go. No one to bitch at him, no need to worry over the responsibility of providing for a family. But now watching how tenderly David looked at his wife, and how thrilled he was for their new little one, Gavin found himself wondering if he was fooling himself. The thought of his sparsely furnished apartment and his cold, lonely bed sent a small stab of remorse into his chest.

CHAPTER 15

*L*indsey looked around the crowded bar where she and Sara had decided to go to enjoy their night off and smiled. As it happened, they ran into Rachel from the high school café and two of her friends, who promptly invited them to join in on their girl's night out. Lindsey missed getting together with her friends back in her hometown and was happy to join in with the small group. She giggled at an off-color joke Rachel had just told and lifted her nearly empty beer to her mouth. She sputtered and coughed, the last of the cool liquid sliding down her throat when she caught sight of Gavin strutting through the entrance of the bar.

"You okay?" Sara asked, reaching over to pat Lindsey on the back.

Nodding her head and wiping her mouth with a napkin, Lindsey forced her eyes away from the incredibly handsome man she couldn't stop thinking about and looked to the other women sitting around the high-top table next to the dance floor.

"Yeah, it just went down the wrong way," she answered.

It was probably stupid to hope he might notice her and come over. He'd entered the bar alone which meant he was probably on the prowl, already having forgotten her and on to his next conquest. She hadn't seen or heard from him since he'd taken her home and doctored her up a few nights ago. When he came back into view, her troubled heart eased a bit. Instead of finding some random bar bunny, he sat down at a table with one of the paramedics she'd seen at a couple of the accidents she'd had to deal with over the last week while on duty.

"Why so quiet all of a sudden?" Sara asked, nudging Lindsey with her elbow. Feeling a tinge of pink creep up her neck at being caught staring at Gavin, Lindsey turned her head toward her partner. She didn't have to answer when Sara focused on where she'd been looking. "Oh, I see who's caught your attention. You should go ask him to dance."

Lindsey shook her head. What if he refused? She didn't want to take the chance her fears would be confirmed that he was done with her. Not when she was starting to acknowledge she had feelings for him. Turning to Carly who was seated on her other side, Lindsey decided to put Gavin out of her mind. If he wanted something more, he'd have to be the one to initiate things.

"So, I'm dying to know how you met and fell in love with Gage," she said, angling herself toward Carly, one of Rachel's friends, so that Gavin was mostly out of view.

Listening with one ear to Carly tell the story of how she'd met her husband, Gage Wilson, retired quarterback for the Dallas Rattlers, Lindsey tried to not pay attention to what was happening a few tables away. She could still see Gavin with his back turned to her out of the corner of her eye. Despite telling herself she didn't care, he could do what he wanted, she couldn't help the little tinge of satisfaction each time one of the girls that approached him pouted and walked away when he shook his head at them. Maybe he wasn't as promiscuous as Sara had told her.

Lindsey's heart swelled for an instant when Gavin stood up from his bar stool, thinking maybe he would come over, only to deflate when he headed down the hallway to the restrooms. With Gavin out of sight, she turned her attention back to Carly. Just as her new friend got to the part where her ex-husband had kidnapped her, Lindsey sat up straight and a shiver went up her spine. A low throb settled between her thighs when Gavin's deep voice washed over her from behind.

"Evening, ladies."

Lindsey twisted around on the tall stool while the

others returned Gavin's greeting. As she turned, Sara caught her eye. With a smirk, Lindsey's partner gave her a wink. While she'd talked at length to Sara about her feelings for the man now standing behind her with both hands on the back of her stool, she'd been reluctant to take her suggestion to try to rope him in. Lindsey had been adamant that he be the one to make the first move if he was interested.

With her heart beating out of her chest, Lindsey trailed her eyes up his tall frame, not missing the way his muscular thighs filled out his dark wash Wranglers and the paisley-patterned blue button-up shirt clung to his six-pack abs and set off the darker shade of his skin. When her gaze landed on his square jaw and the neatly, trimmed goatee that framed his perfect lips, she startled as he leaned in and kissed her on the cheek and murmured, "Hey, beautiful."

"Hey," she answered, not quite sure what he was up to, but hoping his actions meant he was making a move.

She shivered and placed her trembling hands into her lap at the brush of his lips against her ear. Her heart soared when he whispered, "Want to dance, baby?"

With a nod of her head, Lindsey took his offered hand and ignored Sara's cry of, "You go, girl!" When Gavin placed one hand on her waist and the other grasped her hand, a flood of warmth filled Lindsey's chest.

The way he held her shuffling along to the slow twang of the country song had her floating on air. The fact that he approached her made her believe he was ready to explore what she'd felt since the first taste of his lips—the heady feeling that they were meant for each other.

Dance after dance, no matter the tempo, Gavin continued to hold Lindsey close, filling her heart with warmth and not a small amount of hope. As the song ended and Sara waved to her from across the dance floor, Lindsey lifted her head from Gavin's shoulder.

"Seems I'm wanted," she sighed, taking his hand and leading him over to the table where the rest of the girls had gathered up their purses and jackets.

When Gavin simply followed along, Lindsey smiled. Here he was, the town playboy, trailing behind her like a lovelorn puppy. That is until, he wrapped his arms around her from behind when she reached for her purse and growled, "You're not going anywhere, baby."

Sinking back into his embrace, Lindsey grinned at Sara. "I'm going to stay a little longer."

"Want me to see if Joey will stash that for you some-where? He's the red-headed guy behind the end of the bar. Should I come back and pick you up after I drop them off?" Sara asked nodding toward the small group waiting by the door and reaching for the purse Lindsey handed over.

Sara had volunteered to be the designated driver so the others could all enjoy a drink or two and was taking her responsibility to heart. Even though Sara had encouraged her to go for it if Gavin made a move, she wouldn't leave Lindsey behind without knowing she was in safe hands. Before she could tell her partner she'd be fine and would call an Uber if necessary, Gavin spoke up.

"I'll make sure she gets home, you girls go on home and tell David and Gage 'hello' for me," he said, turning toward the others.

After some quick goodbyes and a couple of reassurances she would be fine, Lindsey found herself once again being led back out to the thinning crowd twirling away to the next song, while the others headed out the door. After a few slow turns around the dance floor, Lindsey found herself yawning, her eyes drooping trying to follow Gavin's lead. While she'd taken a nap earlier in the day after a long night searching on foot for the two thugs who'd once again tried to break into the pack and ship store, she hadn't gotten nearly enough sleep—too ramped up about enjoying her night off.

When Gavin raised her arms to spin her around in the fast-paced song that had started up, she tripped, nearly plunging down on the scuffed-up hardwood floor. Luckily, though, Gavin caught her lifting her up into his strong arms and carrying her over and setting her down on a stool in front of the long wooden bar top. After retrieving her purse from the bartender friend of Sara's, she slid off the stool. Gavin took her hand and led her to the front exit. She ignored the narrowed eyes a few of the skimpily dressed girls who'd tried to get Gavin's attention earlier directed her way. Refusing to acknowledge the fact that he'd probably taken more than one of them to bed before, Lindsey took solace that he'd chosen to approach her, clearly wanting to be with her rather than them.

CHAPTER 16

"*H*ang on. Almost there, baby," Gavin crooned to the sleepy woman clinging tightly to his neck as he easily carried her up the steps to his apartment. Reaching his door, he made quick work of unlocking the deadbolt and stepping inside. His mouth went dry and his heart skipped a beat when she sighed and snuggled closer With a slow grin spreading over his face, he took a couple of long strides across the carpeted floor.

"Where are we?" Lindsey asked as he laid her down on his well-worn leather sofa and flipped on a nearby lamp.

"At my place. I didn't want to rummage through your purse for your keys, so I brought you here."

As she sat up and blinked, he watched Lindsey look around the tiny space that was a mirror image of hers.

"This looks just like mine," she replied, getting up and yawning.

"Remember, I live in the same apartment complex."

"Oh, yeah. How come I never see you?"

"Probably because I work a lot and my place is on the far side of the building across from yours."

"That makes sense. Can I use your restroom?"

"Of course, baby. You know where it is."

While she was gone, Gavin looked around at his worn-out sofa and the small, round dining table with only two chairs and pressed his lips together at what she must be thinking. Here he was in his mid-thirties with nothing much to show for it. He'd never had the desire to impress anyone, only requiring a place to lay his head after a long day's work. If he needed space and more comfort, he could always visit his mom and step-dad in their sprawling ranch-style house on the other side of town.

Standing by the small breakfast bar separating the minuscule kitchen from the living space, Gavin startled when Lindsey's arms snaked around his waist. Instantly his dick swelled almost to the point of discomfort as she rained kisses up his neck to the underside of his jaw.

"Do you want me to stay or should I go?"

He took in a deep breath and looked into her searching gaze. He didn't know. His original thought had been to fuck her once and to get her out of his system and move on to the next one. But things had started to change the more he got to know her. For the first time in his life, he found himself wanting more. But he was still conflicted. He wasn't ready to declare he was falling in love but being around Lindsey was making him reevaluate his life. While he'd always thought he didn't want to be tied down to one woman, the longing in his heart to hold her in his arms and make sweet love to her had opened his eyes. With new perspective, he'd begun to be aware of the surprising number of positive relationships around him. David and Rachel, Gage and Carly, plus a few other guys at the fire department. Was it possible he could have the same with the beautiful woman in front of him?

His heart swelled at the possibilities as he leaned in to nip at her lips. "Will you stay?"

"Yes," Lindsey breathed out on a sigh, pulling his head down to press her mouth to his. Placing a hand on each side of her full rounded ass, Gavin lifted her up and swiftly walked down the short hallway straight to his bedroom, eager to sink into her warmth one again.

CHAPTER 17

$\mathcal{L}$indsey made her way across the common area of the apartment complex, the leaves on the large oak trees overhead rustling in the gentle breeze of the early morning. She'd woken up to find herself in bed once again with Gavin. But in the light of day her earlier doubts had set back in and she wasn't sure what he was after. Yes, he'd approached her the night before, but he'd made no comment on what he wanted from her.

Lindsey gazed into the mirror while she ran a cloth under the warm water. She wrung out the excess moisture then swiped the wet cloth across her face, removing the remnants of the makeup she'd applied the night before. She leaned in closer, tilting her head and raising an eyebrow while studied her reflection.

.   .   .

What was happening between her and the man still sleeping in his apartment so close to hers. Did he want more than a fling?

All the signs were there. Twice now he ignored other women who'd made it abundantly clear they wanted him and had chosen to spend time with her instead. While she was hesitant to pursue a stronger connection with Gavin, she couldn't deny her heady attraction toward him. She'd never before hopped into bed with someone so quickly without getting to know them first. But the longing to feel someone hold her once again had let that conviction fall to the wayside once she'd gotten a taste of Gavin's delicious lips and his oh so perfect cock. Was she making a mistake thinking he might possibly want a relationship?

Her heart wanted to believe he did, but her sensible side told her to be cautious.

And with his reputation preceding him, even if he said he wanted to keep seeing her, how could she ever be sure he wouldn't eventually tire of her. After all, he was used to a variety of women.

. . .

No, better she forget about him and find someone else. The thought he might decide later on down the road that she wasn't what he wanted was almost more than she could bear. Not after going through the devastation of losing John. Better to be safe than sorry.

———

"Looks like you're moving up in the world," Sara said, dangling the keys to the patrol car in Lindsey's face.

"I'm driving today?" Lindsey asked, swiping the keys out of her partner's hand.

"Yeah, Chief Scott thinks you're ready and so do I. You have the experience, but we just needed to go through the steps so there's no question of favoritism down the line."

Lindsey understood what Sara was implying. Once it got out that she was the widow of a fallen officer, every little bit of progress she'd made in moving up the ranks would be scrutinized by her coworkers as to whether she'd been given the step up in sympathy rather than on her own merit. It had been one of the many problems back at her old precinct. Although she wanted to move up, she also worried how it would look to everyone if she did it too fast.

She looked at Sara. "Am I going out on patrol by myself?"

"Not yet," Sara answered, walking around to the passenger side of the vehicle. "I'll be with you for two more weeks, then the chief will reevaluate your status. But don't worry. I have no doubt you'll be out on your own soon. You're an excellent officer and everyone so far is impressed with your abilities to do the job."

Lindsey smiled and got into the driver's seat, relieved to know she was making progress on her own, and that she'd be riding with her partner for a little longer. She'd planned to take Sara's advice and start expanding her options where love was concerned. While she desperately wanted to believe Gavin might be the one, she wasn't going to pin all her hopes on him. Maybe going on a few dates with someone else would clear up the question of whether or not there was something there or her judgement was clouded because she'd been so desperate for a man's touch. If he truly wanted to pursue something with her, he was going to have to say it.

Pulling out of the police station parking lot, Lindsey swallowed the lump in her throat. "So, tell me about your cousin."

"Ah, ready to move on, I see," Sara said, turning in her seat to look at Lindsey.

"Yeah. I think you're right. I need to see who else is out there before I get my heart broken."

"Oh, honey. I know Gavin is every woman's dream, but I think you're better off looking somewhere else. You'll like my cousin. He's an upstanding citizen and runs his own business. Plus, he's a sweetheart. How about I give him your number and you can take it from there?"

"Sure. Sounds great. I can't wait to meet him," Lindsey replied, ignoring the small twinge of pain in her chest at the thought of not being with Gavin again. Something she was sure would happen when he found out she'd gone out with someone else.

Gavin clenched his jaw and sucked in a breath. He focused on Lindsey across the crowded restaurant. He'd come to Rosalita's to pick up the order he called in for the construction crew working late on the latest house renovation Stevens' Construction had started. Seeing her sitting across the booth from Rob Daniels, obviously on a date, had his heart beating heavily in his chest and his fists clenching at his sides. The image of another man's hands touching her delectable body was making his blood boil.

But, at the same time he couldn't fault her. He hadn't said he wanted more. Hell, he hadn't known for certain until this very moment. Pressing his lips together and blowing out a breath of air, he took the two large bags the hostess handed over and went back out to his truck. He had a lot of thinking to do.

CHAPTER 18

*L*indsey looked up at Rob. Her heart fluttered mildly in her chest as he leaned in. When his lips brushed against hers the only thing that crossed her mind was that it felt nice, but clearly lacked the fiery passion she'd felt with Gavin. Thankfully, Sara's cousin soon pulled his lips away and smiled down at her.

"Thanks for the lovely evening. I hope you won't mind if I call you again?"

"Sure, that would be great," she answered, although unsure if she'd go out with him again if he did. She sucked in her lower lip and avoided looking at him as he helped her into her car, the guilt of comparing him to Gavin through-out the night hitting her hard. She needed to get her head on straight.

Driving out of the parking lot, she let out a sigh. Sara's cousin was nice, but there had been no spark.

Not after she'd had a taste of Gavin and the fiery passion he invoked. It wouldn't be fair to Rob, or anyone else, if all she did was think about someone else. No, she either needed to get Gavin out of her head or ask him right out if he had any feelings for her. If he said yes, then perhaps it was worth the effort to take a chance on him and see where things might go. Broken heart be damned if things didn't work out.

Now all she had to do was find a way to let him know. Looking at the time on her phone as she pulled her car to a stop in her assigned spot close to her apartment, she saw that it was still early in the evening. Maybe he was home. Smiling, Lindsey made her way across the common space and around the building to Gavin's apartment. Her lower body began to tingle in anticipation of having him take her in his arms. If everything went the way she hoped, she'd be back in his bed soon.

Her heart was beating out of her chest as she raised her hand and knocked. The door opened and Gavin with his long-sleeved denim shirt unbuttoned and hanging open stood before her. With a whoosh, the air in her lungs rushed out and she nearly went to her knees. The sight of his muscular chest covered by the light dusting of dark hair across the expanse sent a pulsing jolt of need through her core.

After her shaky and breathy, "Hi", Lindsey's stomach plummeted to the ground. The answer to her unspoken question was clear when a beautiful, dark-skinned woman joined him in the doorway.

"Lindsey. What are you doing here? I thought you were on a—"

She didn't let him finish despite the dismay in his voice. She couldn't believe he'd moved on so fast. No, wait a minute. Yes, she could. That's what he did. Dropped one woman and picked up right where he left off with another. Straightening her shoulders, determined not to show him how much she was affected by seeing him with someone else, she smiled. "My mistake. I was just going to ask you a question, but it's not important. I can see you're busy."

Turning on her heel. Lindsey quickly made her way back around the corner of his building all the while ignoring his pleas to come back, that 'it wasn't what it looked like'.

Yeah, buddy. It was exactly what it looked like, she thought, slamming and locking her door. Through the onslaught of tears that began to fall uncontrollably, her phone dinged with an incoming text. Wiping away the moisture on her face the best she could, Lindsey pulled the small device from the pocket of her jeans then walked down the short hall to her bedroom, looking at the screen.

It wasn't what you think. Please come back and let me explain.

With a huff she flipped her phone to vibrate and placed it face down on the nightstand by her bed. There was no sense in responding to Gavin's text. He would get the message soon enough. After several minutes, the small hum from the numerous messages he was sending stopped. With a sigh, Lindsey changed into her favorite over-sized sleep shirt and crawled underneath the fluffy comforter. She'd been a fool to think she and Gavin had had a chance. He was never going to change his ways, and she was better off without him.

CHAPTER 19

Gavin watched in disbelief as Lindsey hightailed it around the corner of his building. He would have chased after her, but he didn't want to leave Tamera alone in the state she was in. She'd caught her latest boyfriend with another woman and was threatening to get back at him. His sister was hot-headed, and he needed to make sure she wasn't about to do something she'd regret later or worse get her arrested.

"You should go after her," Tamera said as she turned and moved back over to the breakfast bar. Picking up the glass of water he'd handed her before Lindsey had shown up at his door, she took a long drink.

"I'll talk to her later. Right now, I need to make sure you're going to be okay." Gavin gave his younger sister a quick grin and a wink despite the heavy feeling in his gut remembering the devastation on Lindsey's face when Tamera had come up beside him at the door.

"I'll be fine and don't worry. I'm not going to do anything. I'm better off without him. Thanks for listening, big brother," Tamera murmured in his ear, giving him a kiss on the cheek and setting her empty glass down on the bar.

"You're welcome that's what I'm here for. Are you really okay?"

"Yes. Now you better promise me you're going to go after that sweet girl It's high time you settled down, and she looked perfect for you."

Gavin looked deep into his sister's eyes so much like his own. Satisfied she was being honest and the crazy 'I'm going to kill him' look was gone, he nodded his head. "Yeah, I'll talk to her. I'm not sure where things are going, but she's different."

Picking up her purse, Tamera gave him a wide smile and headed for the door. "I better get the lowdown on her soon."

Gavin shook his head and chuckled. "Love you, sis, but you need to mind your own business."

"Fine. I love you, too," Tamera said as she reached for the door.

Once his sister had shut the door behind her, Gavin finished stripping off the work shirt he'd been changing out of. He walked across his small living space to pick up his cell phone lying on the small breakfast bar. After grabbing the T-shirt he'd thrown across one of the bar stools and pulling it over his head, he looked to see if Lindsey had answered his text. She'd read it but had left no response. He pulled up her number to call her. With his thumb hovering over the screen he hesitated. She probably wouldn't answer. He hadn't missed the utter look of despair on her face when Tamera had joined him at the door. *If only he'd been alone when she showed up.* Obviously, her date hadn't gone well, otherwise she would have still been out with Rob, possibly even in his bed.

Deciding he should go over and make her talk to him in person, Gavin headed for the door. Reaching for the handle, his phone buzzed and vibrated in his hand. Looking at the screen hoping to see Lindsey's name and face he frowned. Instead of her beautiful visage, David's ugly mug popped up. Opening the door and stepping out, he answered.

"What's up?"

"Hey man, glad I caught you. I hate to ask, but we've got a water leak at the new project. Do you think you could go help Charlie out? He stayed to finish the tile work and discovered it when he was about to leave. I'd go but the twins caught a stomach bug, and I don't want to leave Rachel here alone to deal with them."

Holding the sigh in his throat back, Gavin fished his keys out of his pocket and headed to his truck. "Sure, no problem. On my way, I'll let you know when it's fixed. Take care of those kids."

With going to Lindsey's out of the question for the

moment, Gavin ended the call with David then pulled her name back up. After climbing into his truck, he sent off a series of texts to her. Even though she might not read or answer right away, his words would be there regardless. She'd read them eventually.

CHAPTER 20

*L*indsey tried to put what happened with Gavin out of her mind, but try as she might, Gavin's texts from the night before kept swirling around in her mind. Focusing on the road ahead as she drove the patrol car, she reflected on his words.

Please, believe me. The woman in my apartment is my sister, Tamera. I would have come after you, but she just broke up with her boyfriend and I didn't want to leave her alone. After she left, I was headed over to talk to you, but David called with an emergency at our latest renovation.

I saw you with Rob Daniels and want you to know that I came to realize something. I think I'm falling for you. I wanted to tell you that in person, but I know you were upset when you left.

God, I hope you're feeling the same way, and that's why you came by. Anyway, if it's not too late,

I'll come over when I'm finished, and we'll talk. If that's okay?

She'd been incredibly upset, but now she didn't know what to think. Was the woman really his sister? Thinking back to the encounter, she recalled the woman that had appeared at Gavin's side. She couldn't deny that their eyes had held a similarity—both in shape and the same mix of brown with flecks of green framed by long thick lashes. If he wasn't lying, should she give him another chance? Turning to her partner, she opened her mouth to ask if he had a sister only to be interrupted by dispatch calling for them on the radio.

"Dispatch to Unit nineteen."

Lindsey watched Sara retrieved the radio controller from the dash. "Unit nineteen. Go ahead dispatch."

"Ten-forty at twenty-two nineteen Pine Avenue."

Lindsey quickly dismissed her thoughts of Gavin. A ten-forty indicated a robbery in progress and the address was one she and Sara were familiar with. Twenty-two nineteen Pine Avenue was the address for the pack and ship store that had previously been broken into. Being only a block away there was a very good chance they would be able to catch the perps who had been seen around the strip mall in action. Lindsey whipped the patrol car around while Sara talked to dispatch.

Once she reached the alley behind the businesses, Lindsey turned off the headlights and eased down the gravel strip until they were behind the hair salon next to the pack and ship store. Easing out of the car, she turned on the radio clipped to her right shoulder. After adjusting the volume to minimize the chances of being overheard by anyone inside, Lindsey followed behind Sara as she slunk along the back of the brick building to the rear door standing slightly ajar.

Pulling her service revolver from the holster, Lindsey stepped forward as Sara motioned for her to follow her inside after checking that the back entrance was clear. As quietly as possible they made their way through the hallway crowded with boxes ready to be shipped. Hearing a muffled noise and a, "Watch it," coming from somewhere ahead, Lindsey moved behind Sara to the front of the store.

Stepping over a couple of boxes that had been ripped open and the contents scattered across the floor, Lindsey and Sara continued to the open door of a small room behind the lobby of the store. From her vantage point she could see at least two scrawny guys in hoodies and faded jeans hanging loosely on their hips steadily ripping open boxes, stuffing anything of value into the large duffle bags laying at their feet. Lindsey tightened her grip on her service revolver and let out a deep breath as a wash of bright lights flooded the entrance of the store from the patrol cars arriving to answer the call for back-up Sara had sent out.

Confident she and her partner could get the situation under control, Lindsey looked to Sara who nodded her head in silent acquiescence. Taking a deep breath, Lindsey took a step forward aiming her revolver at the nearest intruder and shouted, "Stop. Police."

The young man turned to her, his mouth dropping open and his eyes widening. Lindsey was caught off guard, though, when a third intruder she'd failed to see behind a tall stack of boxes whipped a gun from out of his waistband. Before she could step back, a searing pain tore through her upper arm. Staggering back, she fired off a shot. The bullet hit the front window shattering it into a million tiny pieces, and Lindsey swore under her breath.

Sinking to the floor as Sara called into dispatch to report an officer down and needing assistance, Lindsey chanced a look at her arm. Bile crept up her throat at the sight of a gaping wound in her bicep with blood flowing freely down her arm.

At the sound of gunfire coming from the front of the store, Lindsey knew the perpetrators were trapped. Between the officers out front who'd arrived just in time, and she and Sara in the hallway leading to the back, they had nowhere to go.

She sent up a silent prayer that everything would be under control quickly. Until then, the blood streaming from her arm needed to be stopped. Looking around she found a roll of tape used for sealing up boxes that came into the store. With Sara's help, she managed to wrap a length of the sticky material around her arm just below the shoulder staunching the flow considerably.

A little light-headed, Lindsey slumped against the wall. Helpless to assist, she watched Sara return fire as one of the robbers tried to shoot his way past them.

CHAPTER 21

Gavin guided the fire engine down the alley, following the ambulance as they made their way through the narrow space behind the row of stores. Normally, he and David wouldn't have gone along on the medical call, but with the situation so volatile, the whole crew was on scene in case more hands were needed. While he'd been concerned upon learning an officer was down, his worry increased tenfold when he spotted Lindsey and Sara's patrol car in the alley, easily identified by the unit number on the back of the vehicle. He wouldn't know who was injured until the medics could get inside. With his heart pounding, he stopped the fire engine behind the ambulance two doors down from the pack and ship store where the robbery was taking place.

They would have stationed themselves several blocks away until the scene was secure, but dispatch had said the injured officer was in danger of bleeding out and they needed to be closer, if possible, in order to get to them was faster. Lowering the driver's side window of the fire engine a few inches, Gavin flinched, his heart beating out of his chest at the sound of gunfire coming from inside the building. Looking to his captain, he gripped the steering wheel, trying to keep himself from leaping out of the cab and rushing inside. The image of Lindsey lying inside, injured and in danger of losing too much blood, was almost more than he could handle.

"What should we do?"

"Hold tight for a few more minutes. Hopefully, they'll get everything under control and the ambulance crew can get inside," David replied, his lips pressed together, the radio firmly in his hand.

Gavin lasted two whole minutes before the situation got the better of him. In that instant he knew he couldn't live without her. Somehow over the last few weeks she wormed herself into his heart, and the thought of her dying before they could get to her had him shoving open the fire engine door and leaping out.

Ignoring David's order to get back inside the truck, knowing he'd be reprimanded for his actions, he slunk along the brick wall of the buildings until he reached the backdoor of the store. Not letting the sound of gunfire deter him, he inched his way around the slightly open door and eased inside.

Sticking close to the wall, Gavin hunched over to

minimize the chance of becoming a target. He slowly made his way down the hall, stepping over a few boxes that had fallen to the floor. Coming to a stop next to an open door, his heart seized in his chest. Lindsey, in her police uniform, one sleeve soaked in blood, sat with her back leaned against the wall, her eyes closed. Next to her in a crouch with her gun in hand was Sara, her eyes trained on the open door leading to a room full of boxes.

Taking a deep breath, Gavin dropped down to his hands and knees and crawled toward the pair. At the scuffle of his boots on the floor, Sara turned toward him. With a nod of her head and a finger pressed to her lips reminding him to be quiet, she allowed him to pull Lindsey toward him. Quickly and quietly, he moved her across the tile floor until he had her in the hallway.

Just as he was about to check her vitals, a hail of gunfire burst through the open door. Abandoning his plan of picking her up and scurrying out the back, he dropped back down and covered her with his body. He lay there, listening while Sara and the other officers got control of the situation. At the sound of handcuffs snapping shut, the tension in his shoulders eased a bit.

Gavin bowed his head and let out a deep sigh as Lindsey's breath brush across his face. For a brief few seconds his heart had stopped in his chest when she hadn't made a sound as he moved her across the room. Now the only thing on his mind was helping her. With his stomach churning he scooped her up and headed for the back door.

And he damn sure wasn't going to let her out of his sight.

CHAPTER 22

*T*hrough the sound of muffled voices and then the light thump of a door shutting, Lindsey roused, awaking from her deep slumber. As her mind cleared, she became aware of a dull ache in her right arm.

Opening her eyes, she blinked, looking up at a stark white ceiling. The steady *beep, beep* of a machine caught her attention. She turned her head to the side. She squinted her eyes until a monitor with upside down v's pulsing in a steady beat across the screen came into view. Lindsey let out a quiet exhale and pushed her head into the pillow on the hospital bed, giving thanks she'd made it through the whatever had put her here. Startling when a cool hand grabbed her own, she quickly turned to her other side. With her vision clearing a little more, a nurse in purple scrubs came into view.

Smiling the nurse wrapped a blood pressure cuff around her arm. "Glad to see you awake. You gave us quite a scare there for a little while."

"What happened?" Lindsey rasped out, her throat feeling raw and scratchy.

"Well, you were shot in the arm and the bullet nicked an artery. You lost quite a bit of blood. Lucky for you, the brave firefighter who's been by your side all night went in and pulled you out just in time."

Lindsey nodded, her heart soaring that it might have been Gavin who'd stayed with her, although she was afraid to think about what it might mean. Was he just being nice, or did he really mean the things he'd said in the texts he'd sent? Had she answered him like she'd meant to after talking to Sara while out on patrol?

While the nurse took her vitals, she searched her memory, vaguely remembering the call coming through for a burglary in progress, and she and Sara entering the building. She also remembered getting shot in the arm, and Sara helping her slow down the bleeding but everything else was a blur.

After the nurse finished checking her bandage and made sure she was comfortable, Lindsey closed her eyes. Before she could drift off to sleep, the door clicked, and her eyes flew open again. The dull pain in her arm faded away. She took in Gavin's handsome face and tall muscular body as he walked over and placed a hand on the lower part of her leg. She melted a bit inside at the way his lips tipped up and his deep voice washed over her.

"Hey, beautiful. How are you feeling?"

"Better now that you're here," she whispered against the pain in her throat, grinning back at him.

When Gavin pulled his hand away and the smile fell from his, lips Lindsey sighed, her heart heavy in fear she'd said something wrong. She watched with bated breath as he reached for the uncomfortable standard-issue hospital chair and pulled it next to her bed. She swallowed the lump in her throat when he perched on the edge of the seat and reached for her hand. Lindsey waited patiently while his warm, brown eyes scanned her face. The look on his face when his lips tipped up into a smile helped to ease some of her anxiety. She didn't want to be alone, not with thoughts of what could have happened if Gavin, whom she assumed was the firefighter the nurse had mentioned, hadn't entered the building during the gunfight to save her, running through her mind.

Finally, Gavin cleared his throat, breaking the silence that had overtaken the room. "I...I...," Gavin started to say only to stop and clear his throat again. "What I want to say is..."

Lindsey held his gaze and waited when he paused again.

"I don't know if you read my texts, but I think I'm falling in love with you."

The sound of the monitor beside the bed announced

Lindsey's response as the steady beep began to speed up. With her heart swelling in her chest, she smiled at the words she'd longed to hear from the handsome man looking at her with his eyes shining brightly.

Swallowing hard against the pain in her throat, she managed to croak out, "Yes, I read them, and I..." Squeezing Gavin's hand which still had a firm hold on hers, Lindsey's throat tightened and her voice gave out. She recalled the words he'd written. Her pulse pounding while remembering the way he'd confessed he was falling for her.

Lifting her other hand to her neck, she swallowed past the pain again, but nothing came out.

"Here, maybe this will help. Your throat's probably sore from being intubated in the ambulance when you stopped breathing and during surgery while the surgeon patched you up," Gavin said, releasing his grip before he reached over and poured some water into a Styrofoam cup from the plastic pitcher on the rolling table next to the bed.

Lindsey took a couple of small sips of the cool water through the flexible straw, her heart still racing from the proclamation Gavin had sprung on her. With her throat feeling a little less raw, she laid her head back down.

Just as she opened her mouth to apologize for jumping to conclusions when she'd gone to his apartment, Gavin interrupted her. "Don't talk. I can tell how you feel from the look in your eyes. We have plenty of time to figure out where things go from here. Get some rest. We'll talk later. Your parents will be here soon."

Lindsey nodded and closed her eyes, reveling in the feel of his thumb sweeping back and forth across the back of her hand. Drifting off to sleep, she gave silent thanks to John for leading her to someone she could spend the rest of her life loving.

CHAPTER 23

*L*indsey sat the heavy box full of kitchen items down on the counter. It had been several months since she'd nearly died from being shot in the line of duty, and Gavin had declared his feelings for her. Not once had he wavered in his love. She had no doubts he was sincere, and her heart was filled with joy that their love had only continued to grow stronger with every passing day.

Lindsey sat down on one of the new bar stools she and Gavin had picked out a few days earlier when they'd gone furniture shopping to fill their newly renovated house. She cupped her chin in her hands, propped her elbows on the breakfast bar, and looked over to the window above the kitchen sink.

She gave a start when the plant she'd placed there the day before caught her attention. Sliding off the stool, she moved toward the plant from John's funeral only to be stopped by Gavin. Lindsey sighed and sank against his chest as he wrapped his arms around her from behind.

"Penny for your thoughts," he said, dipping his head to place a kiss behind her ear.

"I was just thinking about *us* when I noticed the plant in the window."

"Isn't that the one you saved from John's service? The one you've been trying to get to bloom again?"

Lindsey nodded her head then pulled herself from Gavin's embrace and continued to walk to the window. Reaching out with one hand, she traced a finger along the edge of the white bloom standing tall and strong in the center of the peace lily.

"Yes, it is. I don't understand why it's blooming now."

"Maybe it's a sign from John. You know, telling you he's happy for us."

Lindsey leaned back into Gavin's waiting arms. "I think you're right. This is what he wanted. He wanted me to find someone who would love me just as much as he did."

Lindsey tore her eyes away from the simple white bloom and turned when Gavin pulled away. Her eyes opened wide as he reached into the pocket of his low-slung jeans and went down to one knee.

"I was going to wait until later tonight when we went to dinner, but I think now is the perfect time."

A lone tear rolled silently down her cheek at the

love shining in his eyes and the sparkling ring he held between his thumb and forefinger.

"Lindsey, I never knew what was missing until you came along. My heart beats for you and only you. You're beautiful inside and out, and I can't imagine life without you. You've made me yearn for things I've never thought I wanted—a home filled with love, children to cherish, and a long happy life growing old together. I love you. Will you marry me?"

"Yes," she answered as Gavin slipped the platinum gold ring with a gorgeous solitaire diamond in the center onto her finger. "I love you, too."

As Gavin stood and took her into his arms, Lindsey looked to the windowsill.

Thank you, John.

AFTERWORD

Thank you so much for reading Loving Lindsey. I hope you enjoyed it.

Other books by Larissa Gail

<u>Coaching Carly</u>
<u>Rescuing Rachel</u>
<u>Stirrups and Stockings</u>

To get the latest updates on new releases and sales, sign up for my newsletter here:

Https://www.larissagailromance

I'd love for you to follow me!

https://www.facebook.com/larissagailauthor/

https://www.instagram.com/larissagailauthor/

https://www.goodreads.com/larissagail

https://www.bookbub.com/profile/larissa-gail-
2b2e7f38-1e6a-4fd5-949a-c77af8e9bc52

https://www.facebook.com/groups/
318493105685622/?source_id=399415327148193

ACKNOWLEDGEMENTS

To my wonderful husband: Thanks for believing in me. You know you're my inspiration!

To my editor, Anja. Thank you for you guidance and encouragement. My stories wouldn't be the same without you.

To my friends and family: Thanks for all of your support snd helping spread the word about my books.

To my readers: Thank you, Thank you, Thank you. I appreciate you more than you know!

ABOUT THE AUTHOR

Larissa Gail writes steamy contemporary romance. A lover of coffee, chocolate and a good romance, she lives in Texas with her husband and their fur baby, Moxie. When not writing about hot alpha men and the women who capture their hearts — or even when she is — you can often find Larissa and her husband traveling the country and exploring the great outdoors.

Made in the USA
Coppell, TX
25 April 2021